Barry Crump wrote his first ~~book~~, *A Good Keen Man,* in 1960. It became a ~~bestseller, as did his~~ numerous other books which followed. His most famous and best-loved New Zealand character is Sam Cash, who features in *Hang on a Minute Mate*, Crump's second book. Between them, these two books have sold over 400,000 copies and continue to sell at an amazing rate some 30 years later.

Crump began his working life as a professional hunter, culling deer and pigs in some of the ruggedest country in New Zealand. After the runaway success of his first book, he pursued many diverse activities, including goldmining, radio talkback, white-baiting, television presenting, crocodile shooting and acting.

As to classifying his occupation, Crump always insisted that he was a Kiwi bushman.

He published 25 books and was awarded the MBE for services to literature in 1994.

Books by Barry Crump

A Good Keen Man (1960)
Hang on a Minute Mate (1961)
One of Us (1962)
There and Back (1963)
Gulf (1964) – now titled *Crocodile Country*
Scrapwaggon (1965)
The Odd Spot of Bother (1967)
No Reference Intended (1968)
Warm Beer and Other Stories (1969)
A Good Keen Girl (1970)
Bastards I Have Met (1970)
Fred (1972)
Shorty (1980)
Puha Road (1982)
The Adventures of Sam Cash (1985)
Wild Pork and Watercress (1986)
Barry Crump's Bedtime Yarns (1988)
Bullock Creek (1989)
The Life and Times of a Good Keen Man (1992)
Gold and Greenstone (1993)
Arty and the Fox (1994)
Forty Yarns and a Song (1995)
Mrs Windyflax and the Pungapeople (1995)
Crumpy's Campfire Companion (1996)
As the Saying Goes (1996)
A Tribute to Crumpy: Barry Crump 1935–1996 is an
anthology of tributes, extracts from Crump's books,
letters and pictures from his private photo collection.

~urrently (1997) in print.

WARM BEER

AND OTHER STORIES

BARRY CRUMP

WARM BEER

AND OTHER STORIES

Illustrated by Tony Stones

Hodder Moa Beckett

For Alan,
my son

First published in 1969 by A.H. & A.W. Reed

This edition published in 1997

ISBN 1-86958-550-X

© 1969 Barry Crump

Published by Hodder Moa Beckett Publishers Limited
[a member of the Hodder Headline Group]
4 Whetu Place, Mairangi Bay, Auckland, New Zealand

Typeset by TTS Jazz, Auckland

Photo: NZ Picture Library

Printed by Wright & Carman (NZ) Ltd, New Zealand

Contents

Chapter		Page
1	Crossed Wires	9
2	Double Scotch	16
3	Chelsea's Boat	20
4	Lawful Excuse	25
5	Twice Bitten	36
6	A Bit of a Break	45
7	Trap	55
8	Sewing-machine	63
9	Taxi	69
10	His Just Deserts	83
11	A Clean Swap	93
12	Wharf-and-Rail	105
13	Flower Arrangement	127
14	A Stroke of Luck	134
15	Overheard in the Pub	145
16	Hot Stuff	149
17	That Way	156
18	Horseplay	167
19	Warm Beer	176

This stuff was written during the past few years. Some of it gave me hell to write and some of it was fun. It'll all probably read about the same.

Acknowledgments are due to *Mate*, *Man*, and *New Zealand Listener* and *New Zealand Weekly News*, in which publications some of these stories have previously appeared.

ONE

CROSSED WIRES

Everyone on the line knew that when their 'phones rang medium-long-short-medium-long-short — *dit*, it was Bert Shallcross ringing up Ernie Piper (on short-short-long) and the line was going to be engaged until someone chipped in and asked them to clear it for an urgent toll call.

Bert's wife Betty usually had to ring up anyone else because whether Bert tried to get Sam Dryland on short-long-long or Ray Hope on long-short-short-long or the store on short-long-short or the exchange on one long the result was always exactly the same, and if Ernie wasn't home Bert would often have to crank out his urgent summons half a dozen times before someone answered.

Ernie heard Bert ring as he came in from the shed, and he stepped carefully across the freshly-scrubbed kitchen floor in his gumboots to the phone in the hall.

"That you, Tom?" Bert shouted in his ear. "I think this blasted phone's playing up again. I've been trying to get through to you for I don't know how long."

"That you Bert?" said Ernie.

"Ernie! How the hell did I get on to you? I've been trying to get hold of Tom Cleaser all bloody morning. Been getting wrong numbers all the time, either that or no reply at all."

"Sounded like my ring that time," said Ernie.

"You're short-short-long aren't you? I've been ringing Tom on two longs. There must be something wrong with this bloody telephone again."

"Hang up and I'll try and get through on this phone," said Ernie. "You listen in after I've rung and see if Tom answers. If he does I'll hang up and you can talk to him."

"You want me to hang up?" said Bert.

"Yeah, just till I ring Tom's number."

"Righto then, I'll hang up now."

Ernie rang two longs, and Tom Cleaser's boy answered, "Eight five seven M."

"That you Ivan? Ernie Piper here. Is your dad in?"

"He's out in the shed. I'll get him for you."

"Yeah, tell him Bert Shallcross wants to get hold of him, will you?"

"Mr Shallcross?"

"Yeah, his phone's crook. I'm ringing for him."

"I'll get Dad," said the boy. "Just a moment."

"You there Bert?" said Ernie.

No answer. Bert hadn't lifted his receiver again.

"That you Bert?" said Tom Cleaser. "What can I do for you?"

"Ernie Piper here, Tom. Bert's been trying to get in touch with you but his phone's playing up. I told him to hang up while I rang through for him but he hasn't come back on the line."

"The line might be crook between Docker's place and the bridge again," said Tom. "Ill give him a try from here. What's Bert's ring?"

"D," said Ernie. "A long and two shorts. Ring us back if you have any trouble and I'll try him again from here."

"Okay, I'll do that. How's the herd?"

"Not bad for this time of year. Sent in just over eighty gallons this morning."

"Good. Well, I'll try and get on to Bert and see what he wants."

"Righto," said Ernie.

"Righto," said Tom.

Ernie hung up and put the porridge on. Bert's ring went three times while he was setting the table and then Ernie's short-short-long interrupted him stirring the porridge.

"That you Tom?" he said.

"That you Ernie?" said Tom. "Can't get any answer from Bert's number. The line must be crook all right."

"Sounded okay when I was talking to him before."

"Might be between here and Bert's then," said Tom.

"Tell you what — I'll try him from here again. If I get hold of him I'll tell him you tried to contact him anyway. If it's anything I can pass on, I'll ring you back."

"Okay. Let's know how you get on."

"Righto Tom," said Ernie.

"Righto," said Tom. "Sorry to trouble you."

"She's right. Just hope it's nothing urgent, that's all. Bert sounded a bit worried."

"Well, we'll just have to keep trying, that's all."

"Okay, I'll let you know if I have any luck."

"Righto," said Tom. "I'll stay handy just in case."

"Righto," said Ernie.

He rang Bert's number, ate his porridge, and tried again. No reply. So he rang Tom back.

"That you Tom?"

"That you Ernie? How'd you get on?"

"No good. There's no reply from Bert's number at all. It looks like his phone's out of order."

"That's what it'll be all right," said Tom. "The line's as clear as a bell everywhere else. I've just been talking to Arthur Royle out at Broadford and there's nothing wrong with *his* phone."

"I'd better ring exchange and tell them Bert's phone's out of order. Then I'll drop over to Bert's place and let him know what's going on."

"Good idea," said Tom. "Let's know how you get on. And if you see Bert, tell him I'll be around here all morning, will you?"

"Okay, I'll tell him. Righto."

"Righto," said Tom.

Ernie rang the exchange and reported the breakdown. After he'd carefully cleaned up in the kitchen and wiped the floor where he'd been walking, he got out the tractor and drove down to the creek, crossed into Bert's creek paddock on the fallen willow and walked up the hill to the house. Betty was down at the cowshed but she didn't see him, and there was no sign of Bert anywhere around the house. Ernie stuck his head inside the kitchen door to yell out if Bert was inside and he was just closing the door again when the phone in the passage rang his own ring. So he went in and answered it.

"That you Ernie?" said Tom.

"That you Tom?"

"Yeah, thought I might just catch you."

"I'm up at Bert's place, as a matter of fact," said Ernie. "I came over to tell him to stay handy. They're sending someone out to have a look at his phone. I heard my ring on Bert's phone so I answered it. I see Betty down at the shed but Bert's not here at the moment."

"That's what I rang about," said Tom. "He turned up here just after we'd hung up last time. Tried to ring you back but there's no reply from *your* phone."

"I've been on my way over here," said Ernie.

"What's Bert doing over there?"

"He gave up trying to get me on the phone. He's here right now. Want to talk to him?"

"Yeah, put him on will you?"

"Righto. Here he is now."

"That you Bert?"

"That you Ernie? Where the hell are you?"

"I'm up at your place," said Ernie.

"My place? I'm over at Tom's. You want to see me about something? I'll be home in about half an hour."

"What happened to you? You were supposed to listen after I rang Tom for you."

" . . . Yeah, well I thought it'd be better to come over and see him personally. You can't rely on that phone of mine."

"Yeah, well I've rung up and told them your phone's out of order. We thought it wasn't ringing but it looks as if it's okay after all."

"You were lucky to get any sense out of it," said Bert. "I was trying for a hell of a time this morning. Gave it up in the finish."

"I'd better get straight on to them and tell them not to come out after all," said Ernie.

"Just tell 'em we found out what the trouble was and fixed it ourselves," said Bert. "I'll ring them from here if you like. It's closer, and Tom won't mind."

"No, I'd better do it," said Ernie. "I know the old tart I was talking to before."

"Okay then. I'll tell Tom what's happening. Are you going to wait there till I get back?"

"No, I've got a bit to do before I go into town. By the way, did

14

you get what you wanted from Tom?"

"No, he hasn't got one. I'm going to give Ray Hope a ring as soon as I get back. Tom thinks he might have one. The one I got off you picked up a bit of number eight wire and stripped a couple of teeth. It's down at the garage, you could pick it up on your way back from town if it's ready."

"Okay. I'll give you a ring when I get back tonight and let you know how it goes."

"Okay. What time?"

"After milking, say about half-past six. You be finished by then?"

"Should be," said Bert. "We'd better make it a bit earlier in case old Linda Forsythe gets talking to that sister of hers in Thames again. We'll never get the line if she does. How about I ring you as soon as I get in from the shed? I'll try and get 'em finished early."

"No," said Ernie. "It might be better if you let me ring you. Just in case."

"Just in case what?" said Bert.

"Just in case your phone starts playing up on you again," said Ernie.

"Yeah, good idea," said Bert. "You ring me, I've been having quite a bit of trouble with that phone of mine lately."

"Righto," said Ernie.

"Righto," said Bert.

Ernie hung up and called in at the cowshed on his way down to the creek to thank Betty for all the work she'd done getting his house cleaned up. Then he went home and got himself cleaned up and shaved. Then he got out the old Hudson and set off on the forty-six-mile drive to Croydon to get married.

TWO

DOUBLE SCOTCH

I dropped the pick the moment I hit the bay and rowed ashore like a man possessed. I hadn't had a drink for days and I was sure going to enjoy this one.

It wasn't unusual for the pub to be open this early in the morning, but it looked as though I was the first customer.

Old Harvey the publican was leaning over the bar beside a drink that looked black in the dimness of the bar-room. Elbows on the bar and his right forefinger pointing straight into the middle of his heavy-rimmed spectacle-lens. The right-hand one.

I stopped and watched. Harvey had flipped his lid at last! He took his finger away from his eye and peered closely at it, turning it round and tipping it this way and that. Then he pointed it back into his eye again and held it there.

Poor sod. It had to happen. No one can drink the amount of grog old Harvey had been soaking up for years without it catching up on him in the finish. We'd all been expecting something like this — we'd had enough warning, goodness knows. But I had no idea it'd start this way.

He removed his finger and began inspecting it again with great concentration. I'd have to go and get someone. The cop — no, better get the cook to come down from upstairs first. She could handle Harvey better than anyone. I could leave her to keep an eye on him while I phoned the cop — and the hospital to get ready for him.

I didn't feel at all like the reviver I'd called in for. The sight

16

of what the grog had at last done to old Harvey put me off completely.

He'd put his end-on finger back in the centre of his eye-glass and was staring cross-eyed and open-mouthed at it.

I thought maybe I'd better not leave the cook alone with him after all. There was no telling what he might do in this state. He might do his block completely at any moment. He might even get violent.

He muttered a broken string of curses. From where I was I couldn't hear what he was saying, except that he was cursing. I looked around the bar-room from where I stood in the doorway. The broom in the corner — he'd have to come out from behind the bar to get at that and I could run for it and raise the alarm. The bar stools — only aluminium frames, but in the hands of a berserk man one of them could be dangerous enough. What about the stuff behind the bar? All that glass! And the piece of wood for donging corks into bottles? If he started swinging that thing around! The scissors on the shelf beside the radio? Suddenly the place was filled with potentially lethal weapons.

He obviously didn't know I was there. I decided to stay and keep an eye on him until somebody came. I began to feel the need for a drink, but I didn't dare move in case he saw me and his deranged mind switched from its present harmless occupation to something more unpleasant.

Then he spoke, peering intently again at his finger.

"Well, come on in, Jack, What'll y'have?"

I stood there not knowing what to do. It sounded as though he knew I'd been standing there all the time. What if he thought I'd been spying on him?

He went on: "I've got one of them on me blasted glasses. It'd

17

drive you mad. It just goes round and round. He won't climb off the glass over the rim and if I take me glasses off I can't see him. If I just squash the damn thing it'll make a hell of a mess!

"Ha! There the little sod is."

He flicked something off his finger with his thumb. It landed on the bar and we watched it hurry across the bar-top and disappear over the edge — an ordinary ant.

"I knew he'd climb on to me finger if I held it there long enough," chuckled Harvey "Now what'll you have, Jack? Double scotch? Right. Sorry to keep you waiting. You'd better have this one with me; I see you've got a touch of the shakes this morning."

THREE

CHELSEA'S BOAT

Chelsea lived in a pair of trousers with one long leg and one short one, and a thing like a handkerchief tied round his neck for protection. When I first met him he was living in a magnificent grove of mangroves on a small swampy island about three miles up the Starkie River in North Queensland. He'd been there for about eighteen months and no one seemed to know what he'd been doing before that — he wasn't too certain himself. He was certain enough, however, about what he was doing on his island. He was building a boat, about a 35-footer, out of mangrove logs.

He already had eleven of the most massive mangrove logs you've ever seen bolted around a huge, partly squared mangrove keel. He was cutting and squaring the logs with a blunt handsaw and a blunter axe, and poling and roping and levering them through the mud to where he had a kind of sloping platform hacked out to build his boat on. Then he'd bore holes through the logs with a long, blunt auger and reef them into place with some long blunt bolts he'd perked from a bridge demolition job somewhere. Sacks of them. He wasn't going to run out of bolts.

There were gaps, plenty of them, about two to three inches on the average. But Chelsea had a lot of confidence in half a drum of washed-up pitch he had lashed in a mangrove tree above high tide. You couldn't help admiring the size of what Chelsea had taken on, but it was almost impossible to imagine the thing could ever be floated.

Chelsea worked very hard and he didn't even stop when he

had visitors. I think I was his only visitor in all the time I knew him; he was over a hundred miles from the nearest road or neighbour. And the only way I could see how he'd got there in the first place was in the 12-foot punt that was sunk on the end of its rope near where he slept on a rough platform of hand-hewn mangrove planks between two mangrove trees.

And while he worked Chelsea used to shout orders to himself and then go and carry them out. I suppose it was because there was nobody else there to do it for him.

I used to anchor out in the river and row over with a bit of tucker for him whenever I went past, and maybe give him a hand to drag a log in. But he didn't seem to care whether anyone helped him or not so I never stayed long. The sandflies were a bit thick and vicious in the swamp there.

It was usually worth calling in on Chelsea because he often had a crocodile or two sharing the island with him and I was getting three dollars an inch for the skins, if they were first-grade. The crocs never seemed to bother Chelsea. By all reasonable standards he should have been taken by crocodiles at least fifteen times.

I went south for the Wet Season and when I returned to the croc rivers I suddenly thought of Chelsea and went up the Starkie to see what had happened to him. He was still there. He'd been slogging away steadily all through the Wet — keeping himself and his boat and gear from being washed away in the floods. There were bits of wire and rope strung all through the mangroves tying things back. He'd worked out an ingenious way of making the fullest use of his odd scraps of rope. He'd tied mangrove poles in the middle to span the distances and just tied each end with rope. There were four rickety platforms wedged up in the mangroves at different levels with bits of gear on. He'd been living on fish and stuff and looked a bit thinner than when I'd last seen him.

All that summer Chelsea worked on at his great project. He built it, log by log, halfway up one knobbly, bulging side. It was starting to look a bit crazy, but Chelsea didn't seem to notice. I tried to get him to row out with me to where my boat was anchored, so he could see it from a distance, but he couldn't spare the time.

Mangrove has never been famous for its straightness and Chelsea was evidently running out of logs that could be shaped and sprung into place. Some of the latest gaps were so wide that he was shaping his offcuts to wedge into them.

It got that way I used to pass up and down the Starkie on the other side of Chelsea's island so I wouldn't have to look. Then, on the last trip I was making up there before the Wet Season hit us again, I decided to drop in and see if Chelsea could be persuaded to come down the coast with me for a spell. And his great boat — The Ark — was gone.

I cruised in as close as I could get the boat and as I went past I saw Chelsea's head sticking out of the water. I thought at first that he was just giving himself a rest from the sandflies, but as I cruised round again he yelled out that his boat had slipped off the bank during a high spring tide and it was lying nose-down under the water. At dead low water, he told me, you could actually see a couple of the ends of the logs. He was dismantling it so he could drag the logs out and reassemble it a bit further up the bank.

I haven't been up the Starkie this year. I've been putting it off.

Haven't heard anything of Chelsea, either. There were a couple of nine-foot floods up there during the Wet. His little island must have been completely submerged at least twice . . . for several days.

FOUR

LAWFUL EXCUSE

H.M. Prison, Stortford. October, nineteen sixty-seven. They'd handed me down eighteen months this time. Breaking and entering with intent, unlawfully on premises, theft, idle and disorderly, and insufficient visible lawful means of support — funny how they can make a simple job like knocking off a factory sound like a major crime-wave. Anyway, there I was, and due for the big one. Preventative Detention, the next time they lumbered me, but it was eighteen months too soon to worry about that at this stage.

For the first three weeks they put me in a four-man association-cell with two other blokes because they were rearranging the system or something. I was a bit anxious to find out what kind of blokes they'd put me in with. It makes a big difference when you're locked up with them eighteen hours a day.

Now anyone who's got a bit behind him'll tell you that there's three kinds of lag. There's the bloke who got himself mixed up with the firm's money, or tickled the peter to get himself out of a jam and got lumbered. He's usually a firstie and takes it pretty hard. He's not likely to come back for another dose.

Then there's the bloke who's been plucked on a job, tried and convicted. He takes it all pretty philosophically and just waits till he gets out so he can pull the same stunt again, without making the same mistakes next time. He usually makes a different one, or a variation on the old one.

And then there's the moaner. He's been framed. A victim of circumstance. He should never have been put in here. It's the bloody cops. His mates put it across him. His wife squealed on him and then ran away with another joker . . .

There was a young bloke and an old bloke in this cell with me, and within ten minutes I knew that this young bloke was going to be a prize example of hurt, outraged and bewildered injustice. I was a bit cheesed off about him because I always like to lie around and think things out when I first get inside. Kind of work out where I went wrong and how to watch out for it in the future. And with this bloke pouring out his troubles it was impossible to do anything but not listen as politely as possible. The old bloke had obviously heard it all before and after we'd given ourselves a knock-down to each other he didn't show any interest in anything but a book he was reading.

Young Johnny was an Irishman. He'd been in the country three years and in jail for nearly two of them. Second time inside. Car conversion both times. And both times he'd been framed. They usually start off with something like: "What have the bastards pinned on you, mate?" They think that because they're innocent, everybody is.

"What have the bastards pinned on you, mate?" Johnny asked me as soon as I'd got settled on my bunk.

"Plucked me on a job with a load of hot stuff on me," I told him. "This is my seventh stretch," I added, just to make sure he got the message.

Well, I got the works. He'd been an apprentice jockey — one of the best in the country at the time — and one night he was walking back to the stables where he worked when one of his mates pulled up in a flash car with his girlfriend, hopped out and asked Johnny to watch the car for a minute. They'd be right back and give him a lift home. Johnny sat in the car to wait and next thing round the corner comes a prowl-car. His mate had nicked off and jacked up an alibi and Johnny got a year in boob for pinching the car.

He was done in his career as a jockey and when he came out he was going around looking for a job. He was walking along the street when his overcoat he'd got off the Discharged Prisoners' Aid people blew out and caught in the rear-vision mirror on the front of a car that was parked there. He tilted the mirror back into place and left a perfect thumbprint on it. The cops picked him up a couple of hours later. The car had been stolen and abandoned. He'd got two years this time.

Johnny rambled on about crooked lawyers and the cops beating up blokes in the cells and things like that, till old Charlie on the bottom bunk told him to put a sock in it.

Charlie was a different proposition altogether. I suppose that if it wasn't for him and me teaming up against Johnny's consistent bitching about the food, the officers and everything in general, we'd never have got to be mates. We managed to freeze him into silence whenever we'd had enough of it and it wasn't long before we got to playing cards and swapping books. Charlie wasn't exactly what you'd call a talkative bloke and it was a couple of weeks before I even found out what he was in for.

Murder. He'd done eight years and still had plenty to do. Killed a bloke with a hammer. Made quite a botch of it, according to what rumours were still floating around. The bloke had taken four days to die. There hadn't been much motive except that Charlie had it in for this bloke and worked in the same building. They'd got on to him straight away. He pleaded guilty and got life. And here he was. A good prisoner — probably get full remission.

It's hard to say exactly when two blokes become mates. Things just drift along and then, without you really noticing it, you're mates. Just like that. It just kind of happens. It's the same when two mates drift away from each other. Charlie was ten or twelve years older than me and a different kind of joker altogether. I suppose it was only the mushrooms that we really had in common.

After they gave Charlie and me a peter of our own each, we still used to manage to see a fair bit of each other. And we were sitting against the wall down in the exercise-yard one day, talking about nothing in particular, when Charlie found out by accident how I'd always had a secret ambition to grow mushrooms. And it turned out that the only thing that Charlie had ever really wanted to do was grow mushrooms, just like me. But his people had had hopes for him and made him go into law instead, and he'd given the mushrooms up for lost.

Now mushrooms are a thing you either understand or you don't. I don't mean eating them — I wouldn't eat one if you paid me — but growing them is a real art. Everything has to be just right. You have to get the right spawn and set it in the right manure in the right soil in the right way at the right temperature for the right length of time. The light has to be right and the moisture has to be right. Then, if you've got all these things right and you can tell a bacterial spot of a mummy virus or truffle before it can be seen by the naked eye, they'll grow for you, provided you've got a special feeling for mushrooms. It's a very dicey business, and here beside me was a genuine mushroom man. As rare as hen's teeth, they are. Charlie was the only one I'd run into in over nine years, ever since they deported an old Danish bloke I'd been planning to go into the mushroom business with.

So Charlie and I spent all our time discussing and arguing about the best kinds of outfit and conditions for mushroom-growing. And after about a year we had nothing left to argue about. We'd thrashed out every possible angle and condition of mushrooms and finally come to more or less complete agreement. Or at least as complete as we were ever likely to get.

It was only a dream really, the best way we could think of to pass the time, but we worked out how we were going into business together, just for a kind of joke or something. And then, a month before I was due to go out, Charlie told me he was coming with me so we could get started on our mushroom factory. I thought he was joking and told him not to get too carried away with false hopes, and it was then that my partner Charlie told me the most amazing "not guilty" yarn I've ever heard.

He'd been twenty-nine at the time and working in the Law Draughting Office as a clerk. The bloke he was working under planted some petty-cash discrepancies on Charlie and, to top it off, fought tooth and nail to get another chance for Charlie to keep his job. Naturally Charlie was a bit hot on him. Charlie knew it was this bloke who stung the peter but he couldn't prove it. He let the bloke know he knew about it and the bloke said that if Charlie didn't watch himself he'd arrange to plant another lot on him, and it'd be jail for sure this time.

Losing the job didn't worry Charlie all that much, he still

wanted to go into mushrooms, in spite of his family. But there was a girl working in the same building who Charlie had a crush on. He wasn't the kind of joker who gets girls very easy and this was the big one as far as he was concerned. She was quite keen on Charlie too, and they were practically engaged, but the trouble was that she cooled off him when the trouble about the petty cash cropped up.

Charlie took her along to see the bloke who done it and begged him to at least tell *her* it wasn't him who tickled the peter. But the bloke raised such a stink that Charlie got a month's notice. So Charlie had it in for this bloke good and proper.

About that time the Government was turfing out the capital punishment caper and Charlie had quite a bit to do with drawing up the new Act. And he discovered that because of someone not watching what they were doing, they repealed the old law before the new one was actually fitted into place.

For about three hours one afternoon there was absolutely no law against murder or manslaughter, and Charlie was the only one in the whole outfit who knew about it.

So he bowled into the bloke who shelfed him's office and clobbered him with a dirty big plumber's hammer he'd got from the basement. As soon as he'd done it he saw how stupid he'd been. He beat it home and waited there till the coppers came and plucked him, the same day. When the bloke pegged out they tried him for murder and handed him down a ten-to-twenty. Charlie never even bothered to use his big defence — that there wasn't any law against clobbering blokes with plumber's hammers when he clobbered this bloke with a plumber's hammer. He must have been pretty upset at the time. And he'd stayed in jail ever since. Reckoned it didn't make any difference about the law. He'd murdered a bloke and deserved to pay the penalty for it. But now that he had someone to grow mushrooms with it was a different matter. He'd just about paid his penalty now anyway.

I didn't quite know whether to believe my old mate at first, but he seemed sure enough. As soon as I got out I dug up a lawyer and told him about Charlie and there not being any law against clobbering blokes with plumber's hammers at the time when my mate clobbered this bloke with a plumber's hammer. It took the lawyer a few days to check up on it. It was the dinkum oil.

They took it all very quietly and sprung Charlie without too much trouble. They didn't want it getting around about the mess they'd made of getting the laws about murder changed. Imagine what would have happened if word had leaked out at the time! I met Charlie as soon as he got out and took him back to the room in a boardinghouse I'd fixed up for us. It was a great day for Charlie.

He was a bit lost at first. Everything had changed while he was doing his ten years. He could hardly recognise the cars and the women and the shops, the roads — just about everything. It was going to take him a few months to get used to things. The only thing that hadn't changed was mushrooms. Once you're a mushroom man, you're a mushroom man for life.

Charlie had a hundred and forty dollars and I did just one small job and got another thirty-five. It wasn't much to start out on, but with a bit of careful handling it might just be made to work. We already had all our plans made, all we had to do was carry them out.

Now blokes like us can't very well bowl up to a bank manager and ask for an overdraft to get started in the mushroom-growing business. We had to be a little more subtle about it.

I found the cellar. It was just right. All concrete, about five hundred square feet of it. The basement of a place where they made ladies' dresses and hats and things. They weren't likely to need the basement. They had plenty of space to work in and for storage, and the door to the basement was boarded up with boxes and crates. I had a terrific struggle with myself for and against helping myself to about ninety bucks in a safe in the office upstairs, but eventually I left it there. We couldn't risk it.

We cleaned up one end of the basement and set up our racks. Charlie had a bit of trouble getting in and out through the transom, so I rigged up an easier and safer way through a storm-drain grating from a street that ran along the back of our premises. I got most of the materials we needed from different places around the city, but I had to be especially careful pulling jobs, now that we were going straight. I wired the basement from leads in the factory upstairs and set up heater-blowers so we could keep the temperature right for our mushrooms. Charlie bought the best white-mushroom spoors he could get and we paid for all our manure and stuff. I got the right kind of soil from one of the compost heaps at the city council nursery. We didn't need much and they never missed it.

We worked at night with torches at first, and then I rigged up a subdued lighting system from the power upstairs. There wasn't much chance of us being disturbed, no one came near the place at night, but we'd often be so absorbed in our work that before we could get out of our factory people would start arriving at the one upstairs. And we'd have to wait and work very quietly all day in the sweltering temperature we'd built up for the mushrooms.

We took to keeping food and coffee in our factory and then I ran into a couple of camp stretchers and installed them so we could sleep there. We gave up the room in the boardinghouse altogether as our mushrooms started coming up. We wanted to be right on the job in case anything went wrong.

One night I had to stop a couple of clumsy kids from knocking off the place upstairs. Scared hell out of them. We didn't want anything to upset things at this stage.

I knew a fair bit about mushrooms, but Charlie was a real master at it. He could tell you the temperature in that basement to within a couple of degrees and check a drop or rise almost before it happened. He knew how many pounds to the tray we were going to get and the day they would be cropped before they even came up. No mushroom-virus would have wasted its time trying to get into our place with Charlie there.

And it was a terrific crop. Those mushrooms grew for Charlie as though they'd been waiting ten years for him to get out of jail. They grew so quick I was flat out trying to get them sold. And that was a bit of a problem. We could only deliver at night. I fixed us up with a few dozen cardboard boxes, but they had to be all painted over because we didn't want our name getting confused with the one which was printed on the boxes. And all this took valuable time we hadn't allowed for. Then we had hell's own job getting our boxes of mushrooms out through the storm-drain grating. I had to open up the factory upstairs in the finish and get them all out that way. You have to be very careful how you handle mushrooms.

But eventually we delivered our first crop of mushrooms, in perfect condition. We're still supplying the same clients today, and a lot more besides. We cleared four hundred and eight dollars on that first crop. It had taken us just nine weeks from the time we sprung Charlie out of Stortford Prison.

We've rented the basement now and put in our own entrance. They've cleared the entrance from the factory above for when we want to get anything big in, but we don't have to use it very often. There's our own sign on the door, very small in case we get too much notice taken of us. It's hard to get out of old habits. There's more to going straight than meets the eye.

We've got one corner of the factory set up for experimental purposes and Charlie thinks he's onto a way to cross white and brown spawn. If we can swing that one we'll be famous. And we've got standing orders for all the mushrooms we can supply. We could expand, of course, but Charlie reckons it's better to put our time and work into quality, and that's what we're doing.

And when we've had another few months at it, we'll be properly established as solid, respectable businessmen.

Anyway, I've made the place burglar-proof.

FIVE
TWICE BITTEN

Clive didn't mind dogs in the least. In fact he quite liked them. Although he'd never actually owned a dog himself he always had a spare scrap or a pat for the odd ones that came sniffing hopefully round the door of his bach from time to time. Neighbours' dogs, mostly. He recognised all of them. They made the place seem kind of domestic somehow.

But this one was different. Nobody seemed to know where he came from or who he belonged to. Clive called him Sadly, because he was a sad kind of dog and it didn't seem right to call a dog as dignified as this just plain Sad. And he had to call him something in order to try and send him away.

But Sadly soon made it plain that he had no intention of being sent away. He moved on to the porch of Clive's bach, where Clive found him when he came home from work one afternoon, and stayed there. He wasn't the kind of dog you throw things at, or kick, or even growl at very convincingly.

Clive didn't take much notice of him at first and Sadly took over the bach, keeping all other dogs and cats away and accepting the scraps Clive gave him as though they were well earned. Then the dog took to following Clive around, ignoring with pointed dignity any attempts to send him away or back to the porch.

That was when Clive started making enquiries about who might own the dog, but even advertisements in the papers failed to bring so much as a rumour about Sadly's past or owner. He

just stayed, and the longer he stayed the more possessive of Clive he became. He'd escort him to work and return home and come back to collect him when he knocked off in the afternoon.

At first it was only tradesmen and salesmen and casual callers Sadly bailed up at the gate with hackling snarls and bared teeth, but he soon graduated to Clive's friends or anybody at all. Their calls naturally became even less regular than ever. Once Clive actually slapped Sadly with a heavy doormat, but Sadly took absolutely no notice of him whatever. He held his ground, bristling and growling, while Lucy Scroates tried desperately to crawl through a hydrangea bush in her best stockings. Her attitude towards Clive was noticeably cooler after that.

Sadly started walking in and out of the hut whenever the door was opened, and soon took up residence on the floor of the little kitchen. He'd become very indignant if he was ever shut inside, though, because he still considered his self-imposed duty of scaring hell out of each and every visitor to be an indispensable service.

On the advice of friends, Clive at last called on the SPCA. They didn't appear to appreciate his problem.

Was the animal homeless?

"Well, not exactly, but . . ."

Was it dangerous?

"Not really what you'd call dangerous. It hasn't actually bitten anybody, but . . ."

Was it sick, or injured?

"No, nothing like that, but all the same . . ."

"Sorry, sir, in that case we can't do anything about it. Have you tried the police?"

The police weren't very helpful either.

"Have you advertised for the owner?"

"Yes. For two days in two newspapers."

"Well, in that case, if nobody comes forward to claim the dog within three months of your advertisements you can claim it as your own property."

"But I don't want him."

"Well then, after the three months are up you can sell it to defray your expenses. It's simple."

"But can't I even give him away?"

"Oh no. You couldn't do that until you've established your ownership of him. You could be charged with stealing him if the real owner comes forward."

So Sadly, who'd been waiting outside for him, followed Clive home and moved his camp to the mat on the floor by the bed, and stayed.

And stayed, and stayed, and stayed.

He ate everything that was given him with a complacent off-handedness that cost Clive fifty or sixty cents a day. Whenever he planned a meal he had to allow for plenty of meaty scraps. Sadly's disapproving stare at a scrapless meal was more than Clive could stand. He took to eating out, until he was seen smuggling scraps out of a restaurant and they searched him, thinking it was their cutlery. Then he was caught slipping bones into his pocket by Lucy's mother, who took them and wrapped them up for him. They didn't really mind but the embarrassment was too much for him and he ate at home again. His coat pockets were getting smelly, too.

Whenever Clive drove out in the car, Sadly sat up in the passenger's seat like a garrulous old man being chauffeured around. This attitude began to annoy Clive and he organised a departure one morning in which he managed to slam the car door before Sadly could dive in. Sadly stood aloofly on the footpath and watched him drive away. Clive felt so ridiculous and guilty about leaving him behind that he turned round the block and drove back. There was Sadly, still standing on the footpath, as though he knew he was being returned for. He stepped into the car with a distant glance at Clive and sat staring out of the window with the air of one who is above communicating with such as Clive.

After a couple of months, Clive got to depend on Sadly for company. Lucy was only allowed out once a week (and twice on long weekends) and very few of his old acquaintances ever came to see him these days. He couldn't take what was by now known as a savage dog anywhere where there were children, or for that matter anybody at all. He'd tried tying the dog up at the gate on one occasion, but Sadly chewed through the rope and followed him into the Scroates's living-room. The collar and chain he'd bought after that had never been used, and never would be, if Sadly's attitude towards it was anything to go by.

Soon it was almost impossible for anyone to get near Clive without being menaced by Sadly, who growled and rumbled restlessly all the time they were talking. And Clive tended more and more to take Sadly's side in the differences of opinion between Sadly and his other friends.

Clive and Lucy were out in the car one Sunday, with Sadly, who'd accepted being temporarily banished to the back seat with very ill grace, drooling sullenly over their shoulders.

"I can't stand this brute of a dog any longer!" Lucy suddenly burst out. "You'll have to get rid of him, Clive."

"He's actually a very nice dog, once you get to know him," said Clive. He was well aware of the scarcely veiled hostility that existed between his Lucy and Sadly.

"I don't want to get to know him," she said, impatiently. "I'm not putting up with it any more, and that's that."

"What's that?" evaded Clive uncomfortably. He had an idea there was an unpleasant scene coming up.

"The way you treat that — that thing. It's disgraceful! Everybody's talking about it. It'll end up biting somebody and then there'll be trouble."

"Sadly wouldn't bite anybody," said Clive defensively. "He only pretends to be savage. He wouldn't hurt a flea."

"Well I'm not seeing you any more until you get rid of it, and that's final. You can take me straight home. I'm not putting up with it another instant."

Sadly drooled moodily over the back of the seat, rolling his yellow eyes between one and the other as they spoke. There was a longish silence.

"Okay then," said Clive, pulling up outside Lucy's place with a resigned drag on the handbrake. "I'll take Sadly down to the vet tomorrow and have him put to sleep. They say they don't feel a thing . . ."

"And have this car cleaned out, too," she said. "I can't afford to have my clothes cleaned every time I go out with you."

She kissed him impatiently through the car window and walked quickly away through her front gate.

Clive took the next morning off work and on the way to the Veterinary Centre with Sadly he turned off towards the local boarding kennels. He'd enquire how much it cost to keep a dog there. He couldn't have him destroyed in cold blood. If only the blasted dog would get himself run over by a truck or something. He reached guiltily over and put his hand on Sadly's rough old head, and got a brief distrustful stare in return. He could afford two dollars fifty a week at the very outside, until some other arrangement could be made.

Six dollars seventy-five it cost him. As he drove away he felt as though he'd betrayed poor old Sadly in a particularly underhand way. He'd soon forget that, he told himself. And Sadly was really better off where he was now, with all the other dogs to play with. Though somehow the idea of Sadly playing wasn't a very convincing one. Still, there would be plenty of things for him to watch for and growl at.

The bach seemed empty without Sadly there. Clive surprised himself talking to the dog once or twice. He was still on the outer with Lucy, though she didn't ask and he didn't say what had happened to Sadly.

As the days went by it got worse rather than better. Whenever he went through the back door, Clive held it open for Sadly. Whenever he got in or out of the car he paused for Sadly to hop in or out. Once he even bought fifty cents' worth of dogs' meat on his way home from work. Every knock on the door reminded him that Sadly would have warned him that someone was coming. Whenever he talked to somebody he noticed that they weren't distracted by, if not actually backing away from, Sadly. And it just didn't seem right. He began to realise that the dog had given him a certain colourful status he'd never had before and didn't have now.

Relations with Lucy didn't improve significantly but this worried Clive no more than the absence of his dog. At the first opportunity on the weekend he drove out to the boarding kennels, feeling as though he'd been away for weeks, instead of five days.

Sadly was sitting on his own in a big pen when Clive arrived with the kennel-keeper. The keeper opened the gate and Clive went in and walked smiling towards Sadly. When he was five or six feet away, reaching out to pat the dear old head, the dog, who'd been disinterestedly watching his approach, suddenly sprang up with a lion-like snarl and snapped at his outstretched hand with several loud, wet skulps.

Clive got such a surprise that he nearly fell out of love with Lucy Scroates. He backed away, horrified, until he was stopped by the corner of the pen, with Sadly stalking stiffly after him, bare-toothed and savage. As soon as Clive stopped, the dog went into a half-crouch, as though preparing to spring at him.

Two men came running and they and the keeper prodded and shoved at Sadly through the netting with long sticks and took his attention off Clive long enough for him to escape from the pen. He was unhurt but badly shaken.

"I — I can't understand it," he said, bewildered. "I've had Sadly for months. He wouldn't do that to me!"

"He's been a bit queer ever since he's been here," said the kennel-keeper, leading Clive away from the pen. "He's getting worse, I meant to tell you before — I'm the only one here who can get near him. We've had to take all the other dogs out of that pen."

Clive looked back. The two men were still securing the gate. Sadly had resumed his pose in the corner of the pen as though nothing had happened.

"Something must have gone wrong with him," said Clive.

"He's not like that at all."

"Dogs sometimes go like that when they get old," explained the keeper kindly. "There's nothing much you can do about it except have them put away. Would you like me to arrange it for you?" he asked. Clive nodded and walked toward his car.

Next morning Lucy Scroates visited Clive and talked to him for about half an hour. It was all off between them.

On Monday he turned in his precarious job as a grease-monkey at the garage. On Tuesday he quit his little bach, and on Wednesday he left for the mountains, to hide away till his broken heart mended.

He never got there; but that's another hard luck story.

SIX

A Bit of a Break

Andy Rogers had never heard of the *Gazette*, nor that his name was quoted in the pages of the latest issue in terms which caused grave misgivings in the hearts of a large number of his business acquaintances. He thought it was just a coincidence that everyone suddenly insisted on his paying what he owed them within an impossibly short time. Letters which had hitherto been merely threatening became positively menacing; creditors who had previously only been firmly insistent were now delivering ultimatums.

The only thing that could possibly be called a coincidence was the fact that the gearbox in Andy's thirty-five-foot fishing boat, *South-Easter*, was down to its last few tortured revolutions. The trouble had started four unprofitable trips ago with a faint whine, and was now screaming for attention, along with his unpaid bills. The only thing he could do was to go out and try to fill his freezer with fish to pay a bit off each account and get parts for the gearbox. And hope for the best.

Andy's deckhand, Manny, who'd been with him for two years, refused to put to sea with the gearbox in that condition, and asked bluntly for what Andy owed him in wages. In defiance of the bank manager's definite instructions Andy wrote out a cheque for Manny's pay, and fuelled and provisioned the boat for a quick getaway, just in case. He was an honest enough man but things were getting a bit overwhelming. There had been some unthinkable mention of seizing his boat to pay off a few hundred lousy dollars, when all he needed was a bit of a break on the fishing. He knew the Barrier Reef as well as anyone in the game, but he'd been having a rough spin with the fishing and the weather and the boat and the store and the bank and the fuel agent and everything and everyone else a fisherman comes into contact with.

All he needed was a bit of a break.

He left the jetty and climbed the path up the cliff to home (rent eighty-five dollars in arrears), his wife, and tea. After the two kids were in bed he told her as little as possible about the strife they were in. She added a few more items to the list of debts which he hadn't remembered, including the fact that they had been refused any more leniency from the storekeeper. This didn't greatly worry Andy because by this time he was well beyond the worrying stage.

Marion was a good woman, take it all round, he reflected. Never complained much and hell of a good with the kids. She didn't care for the sea much, but in a way that was a good thing. She didn't interfere with his boat or his work. Andy was specially thankful for her at this time. The one reliable one when everything and everyone was going against him. He glanced at her as she leaned across the table to take his empty plate. Nothing much to look at — in fact she was so nondescript she'd stand out in a crowd — but she was dependable and loyal, and to Andy that was worth more than anything just now.

"I'll have to get out to the reef and load up with fish, love," he said. "If I get a decent haul we can pay a few dollars off each account and keep them quiet till we get on our feet again."

"Isn't there something wrong with the boat?" she asked. "Manny said . . ."

"Oh, that's nothing. Bit of a whine in the gearbox. It'll hold out for another trip or two — it'll have to," he added soberly. "Anyway Manny's quit — did he tell you?"

"Yes," she said tiredly. "When do you want to leave?"

"I'll get away tonight and anchor on the reef. Should pick up a few mackerel and trout on the trail in the morning. I'll stay out this time till I fill the freezer if it takes me a month."

"I'll get your things ready," she said.

Good old Marion, he thought as she went off into the kitchen to fill his tucker-box. Not a single complaint. Most women would have been wailing and complaining about him never being at home, but not Marion. Good scout.

It took him half an hour to say goodbye to her and another half-hour to carry his things down the steep cliff-track to the jetty. He didn't want to use the road because it meant passing the butcher's place and the butcher might see him and get the wrong idea about him sneaking out of harbour in the night.

Three hours later he dropped anchor behind a rocky islet halfway between the harbour and the outer reef and went below to sleep till dawn. It was a relief to get away from the worry of his creditors. He could almost forget about them out here, and he slept soundly till it was time for him to start work.

He ate in near-darkness to save his batteries, started the motor, dragged in the anchor and tried to ignore the rattle of the gearbox as he motored out of the shelter of the anchorage into a fifteen-knot south-easter with plenty of sting in it. He cut her back to about three knots to nurse the gearbox and looped a rope round one of the wheel-spokes while he went forward to let down the outriggers. It was still a bit early for trailing but he let

out both lines and fussed about with the gloves and gear so he wouldn't notice the rumbling beneath his feet so much.

He whistled, checked the freezer, made up a couple of spare traces, adjusted his course slightly, went forward to check the lashings on the anchor, went aft to roll a smoke, sluiced down the deck and whistled louder, but still the gearbox whined and rattled. He knew exactly what was wrong with it — it was completely shot.

It was fully daylight and he could see the scattered brown of the reef and the eye-blue of shallow water round a sand-cay ahead when he got his first strike. The wire cable snapped taut and the outrigger danced against the rigging. It was a good one. He pulled on the gloves, and skull-dragged an eighteen-pound Spanish mackerel into the killing-pen. A good start. A few more of these would be handy. He clouted the fish with the wooden donger, cut a strip from its silver belly to tie along the hooks on the trace for a lure, and let the line out again.

A mile short of the reef he detoured to circle a low flat islet covered with birds and low scrub which leaned away from the wind in close layers like combed hair. He picked up another good mackerel there, and two more on his way across to the reef.

He trailed close in along the inside of the reef, heading north, and picked up five coral-trout, four more mackerel, two bonito and a turrum by midday. He stopped then to clean the fish and put them in the freezer.

Close on a hundred and fifty pounds of saleable fish in a morning was pretty good going. His luck must have changed. If he could keep this up he'd have a full load in a few days. He ate two bonito fillets for lunch because they wouldn't take bonito at the Fish Board.

Andy's change of luck didn't last very long though. When he went to take off again for an afternoon's trailing he'd only gone a hundred yards when the gearbox gave an extra loud rumble, a graunch, and then a bang that shook the whole boat. He cut the motor, threw out the anchor and went below to see what had happened.

Thick, dirty oil was running out of the cracked cast iron casing. Something had finally come adrift in there and jammed against the side of the box, breaking it beyond any hope of repair.

Andy sat in the wheelhouse for a long time wondering what to do. He was still wondering when it got dark that night, so he had a feed of coral-trout, sat on his bunk and wondered some more.

He had four gallons of fuel for the outboard, just about enough to get him into harbour in the leaky old dory that was lashed to the top of the wheelhouse — providing the weather was okay. Towing the *South-Easter* he wouldn't get halfway. That meant he would have to leave her anchored out there while he went for help, or wait with her and try to signal another boat if one came close enough. But the chances of another boat being in this particular area were slight.

He slept, and during the night the wind dropped so that in the morning there wasn't even a white line of water breaking on the far side of the reef as there had been the day before.

He manhandled the dory into the water, checked and fitted the old outboard, loaded water, food, a bailer and spare fuel, let out more anchor-rope on the *South-Easter* and set off for the mainland, which was represented by a faint smudge of hills in the western distance.

For a while, until it tightened up with the soaking water, the dory leaked alarmingly and he had to bail constantly to keep it from wallowing and taking water over the sides. Then he had trouble with the outboard. Dirty fuel. The trip took him all day and it was well after dark when he tied up at the jetty and stumbled wearily up the cliff towards home and bed. He was too tired even to think about his troubles. Marion would be there.

She was. He heard it before he reached the top of the cliff. Loud music, thumping, singing and shouting and laughter. Someone was having a party.

It was at his place. As he approached he could see people milling in the hall through the open front door.

He stopped by the front gate, puzzled. This was impossible. Marion never had parties.

Then he heard her voice. "I can't leave the kids, you know that. Come back after everyone's gone. And for heaven's sake don't make it so obvious in front of everybody in there. We don't want it getting all over the district. Now let's get back inside before they notice we're gone. And don't drink too much," she giggled in a way Andy had never heard before as they went off towards the house. "I want you sober for later . . ."

Andy stumbled down the cliff to the jetty, and stood there bewildered and unbelieving for a long time.

Some time during the night he filled two cans and the outboard motor tank from a twelve-gallon drum of fuel in his little shed and set off out to the reef.

He reached the *South-Easter* in the late morning, tied the dory at the stern, went below and fell asleep on his bunk.

It was dark when he suddenly woke and remembered. He lay there listening to the familiar comfortable boat noises. The chuckle of water along the hull of the boat near his head and a faint slopping in the bilges — or was it the diesel-tank, or maybe it was in the water-tank. The faint whistle of the wind in the rigging and the *tack — tack — tack* of a loose something or other up on deck.

He woke again in dull dawn daylight and knew at once what he was going to do. It took him some time to find the stub of pencil among the junk in the cabin.

The wind had blown up strongly and the sea was a heavy, swelling mass of seasick green that pitched the dory in all directions as he headed for the coast again.

The *Harbinger*, heading south with a load of fish, passed the *South-Easter* anchored out at the reef and hailed her. They circled her a couple of times while the skipper examined her through his binoculars.

"Looks a bit queer," he said to his mate. "Doesn't seem to be anyone on board. We'd better investigate."

He nosed the *Harbinger* up to the *South-Easter*'s stern and his mate jumped aboard with a mooring-line and made it fast to a stanchion. There was a choking stink of rotten fish from the freezer and a foot of oily water slopped heavily in the bilges and across the floorboards in the cabin.

Everything else seemed to be in order, except for the broken gearbox lying on an oily sack in the wheelhouse.

"Looks like they're in a bit of strife with their gearbox," observed the skipper. "They've probably been picked up and gone in for a new box. We'll pump out the bilge for them and get on our way."

"Funny they should leave the fish to go rotten," said the mate.

"Must have been held up somewhere," said the skipper. "Hang on — there might be a message here."

He moved a tin of treacle from an ordinary writing pad on the cabin table and flicked it open. "Hello, they've kept a bit of a log, by the look of it."

He turned the pages to the last entry. "Looks as though they've been gone over a week. This is dated — hell!"

He glanced quickly through the scrawly writing on the page and then turned back to the beginning.

"Get an earful of this," he said to his mate. They read:

Thursday 18th:

Left harbour late and anchored at Little Island. Gearbox holding out and doesn't seem to be getting any worse. No fishing.

Friday 19th:

Trailed out to reef and fished about eight miles north. Got a few fish but gearbox broke up in afternoon. Will have to wait for help.

Saturday 20th:

No sign of any boats. Took out gearbox to have a look at it. Planetary gears chewed out and gone through casing. No hope of fixing it. Feeling a bit off-colour.

Sunday 21st:

Couldn't sleep for pains in the guts but feeling a bit better in the morning. No boats.

Monday 22nd:

Bad pains in the stomach all night and doubled up with cramp or something. (Later.) Think I've got appendicitis. Stomach very sore and swollen. (Later.) Have to go for help. Try and make it in the dory. Can only walk on hands and feet.

Weather blowing up from S.E. but can't hold out here.

The skipper closed the pad and looked at his mate.

"That's the lot," he said.

"Poor bastard, seems to have been on his own. Wonder who he is?"

"Who he *was*, most likely," said the skipper grimly. "Come on, let's get going. We'll have to report this. I'll put a call out on the radio and we'll scout round towards the coast. But if he's not in by this time I don't give him much of a chance."

They found the dory washed up among some rocks, thirty miles up the coast from where he'd landed.

And Andy Rogers had the break he'd needed. He's doing pretty well for himself too, in the logging business. Calls himself Harvey Wilson these days.

SEVEN

TRAP

The telephone rang. Paul and his wife looked across at it and then at each other. She turned back to her magazine. Paul got up, put his newspaper on the chair, and went over to the phone on the sideboard.

"Hullo."

"Is Mister Paul Cross there?" It was a woman's voice. Quite young by the sound of it. Blurred and indistinct, as though she was speaking from a long way off. He had to concentrate to catch what she was saying.

"Speaking!" he said loudly.

"Do you know Harry Newton?" asked the faint voice.

"Should do. He works for me."

"It might pay you to ask him what he's been up to with your wife over the last few months."

"What? What did you say? Who's speaking?"

The voice laughed. "Do you want me to spell it out for you, you fool? He's been skiting all over the place about it."

"What do you mean? — Who's speaking? — Are you there? Hello . . ."

But she'd hung up.

Paul stood there stunned for a few minutes, listening to the humming in the empty telephone. Then he slammed the receiver back on to the phone as though trying to extinguish what he had heard through it. His wife was looking across at him, frowning.

"Who was that, dear?" she asked.

Still without turning, Paul got a bottle of whisky out of the sideboard cupboard and poured himself a drink. He needed time. Time to think.

"Bring me one if you're having a drink, dear," said his wife. "Plenty of ginger ale, please, and a little ice."

He made the drink and took it across to her.

"Thanks," she said. "You didn't say who that was on the telephone."

"Uh — nobody," he said. " — At least, I couldn't make out who it was. They must have been drunk."

She took the drink with a slight shrug and turned back to her magazine. Paul marvelled at the way she'd carried it off all this time. Of course it was all as plain as day, now that he thought about it. A lot of things she'd said and done lately suddenly made sense. The headaches — the Housie evenings — too tired whenever he wanted to go out, and always wanting to go out when he was too tired. . . .

He needed time. He couldn't think. What do you do when someone rings up and tells you your wife has been cheating on you for the last few months? Harry, eh! Wonder who that girl was? One of the popsies he's always bragging about — just like he's bragging about my wife. . . .

He went to bed and lay there in the dark, the words of the anonymous caller barking around in his head . . . *Harry Newton —* *Ask him what he's been up to with your wife — you dumb fool . . .*

Paul pretended to be asleep when his wife came in about an hour after him and undressed very quietly, in case he woke up and wanted what she preferred to give that slouching young hypocrite who was always so anxious to please him. Already a kind of plan was beginning to take shape. They were going to pay

for what they'd done to him. Nobody was going to get away with anything like that on Paul Cross. He didn't sleep at all that night.

Paul had been at work well over an hour when Harry sauntered into the workshop next morning. They got to work welding up the steel frames for a prefabricated building they were contracting for. At lunchtime Harry told him about a girl he was after. Paul was surprised at how easy he found it to laugh with him.

Harry did exactly what Paul expected him to. As soon as he started drilling the hole in the wall of the workshop Harry came over to see what he was doing.

"What's the hole for, Paul?"

"I want to put a bench in along this wall," said Paul casually. "We'll stick a water-pipe through here and let a sink into the bench to wash up in."

"Good idea," said Harry. "Do you want a hand?"

"Aw, don't think so."

Paul put the electric drill on the floor. "We'll have to cut a piece of pipe to go from the one along the side of the building and put a T-joint in. I'll just nip out and measure how far above the ground this hole is."

He took a rule and went outside. Round the side of the building he picked up one of the steel rabbit-traps they'd welded pins on to for a trapper and quickly set it.

"Poke your finger through that hole, Harry," he called. "I can't see where it is from out here."

Inside, Harry unhesitatingly poked his finger through the hole. And Paul sprung the trap on it, the serrated jaws cracking shut behind the second knuckle.

"Ow! Hell!" shouted Harry. "My bloody finger's jammed! Quick! What's going on? Quick, Paul!"

Paul went inside to where Harry was dancing delicately from one foot to the other with his finger caught through the hole in the wall. He turned his head as Paul came in.

"Paul, quick," he gasped. "My finger's jammed in something outside. Quick! Hell it's hurting."

"You don't say," said Paul, lighting a cigarette.

"What's going on? What have you done? This is no joke, Paul!"

"It sure isn't," said Paul. "It's a bit of a shame really. — It's no use trying to pull your finger out," he went on conversationally, "because somebody's ground the teeth on the trap that's on your finger down on an angle. The harder you pull the deeper they'll cut. You'll tear your finger off before you get it free."

"What are you up to?" shouted Harry. "You're mad! Let me out of here!"

Paul stalked slowly towards him, holding out a sheath knife that shone with a newly-ground edge. Harry watched him come closer, his face white and his lips trembling. Paul went slowly closer. Harry was trying to say something but no sound came from his fluttering lips. Suddenly Paul stabbed the knife into the wall near Harry. Harry let out a hoarse groan as he flinched against the agony of the metal jaws biting into his finger on the other side of the wall.

"See that knife?"

Harry didn't answer.

Paul went on: "If you want to get free, Harry boy, you'll have to cut your finger off. That's what you're going to pay for interfering with other people's property."

"You're mad," croaked Harry. "You're mad! " His voice rose to a shriek. "Let me out of here. Let me go!"

"I'm mad all right," said Paul. "I'm mad about you and my wife, Harry boy. That's what I'm mad about."

"You're crazy. I've never touched her in my life. You hear me? I never touched her. You're mad. Let me out of here. Let me go."

Paul began to laugh.

"You're crazy," yelled Harry. "Crazy — Help! Help! Somebody help!"

"You can shout your head off," said Paul pleasantly. "No one'll hear you in here. Now I'm going to leave your welding-torch going against the end wall there. The place'll go up pretty quickly once it gets started, so you'd better be quick with that knife if you want to get out of it alive."

"No, Paul. No — you wouldn't burn down your own workshop. There'll be trouble. You'll get into trouble. You're making a mistake, I tell you. Give me a chance to prove it. Paul, please."

"There'll be trouble all right," said Paul. "But more trouble for you than me. The workshop's insured. And nobody's ever going to believe your cock and bull story about me making you cut your finger off, just so you can get the compensation."

"No, Paul. No. . ."

Harry slumped against the wall. Paul lit the welding torch and threw it into a heap of cotton waste near the opposite wall to the one Harry was against. Then he left the workshop without another word, closing the door behind him.

Harry heard his car drive away.

It was unusual for Paul to come home this early in the day. As he drove into the street he saw the car parked outside his house. It looked like that flash Ford the land-agent bloke he'd bought the house through brought back from America a few months back. Bit of a slimy bastard, Paul thought. Wife about twenty years younger than he was, and a different bit of skirt in his car every time you saw him. A proper bloody ram.

As he pulled up behind the flash Ford, Paul decided that while he was on the job of dealing with things he was going to enjoy telling this greasy Newton bastard — *Newton!*

Harry Newton . . .

Paul spun the car round and drove frantically back down the road towards the workshop, shouting incoherently as he went.

The workshop was burned to the ground, but Harry Newton escaped. After Paul left him he had managed to hook his foot through the lead on the electric drill Paul had left lying on the floor and lift it to his free hand. Then he drilled a circle of holes in the wall around his trapped hand and pulled out a hole big enough to get the trap through. He sprung his finger free and got the doors open enough to slip through before the smoke got him. Then he stood back from the blazing building among the people who were starting to gather, holding his throbbing hand in his armpit.

The workshop was beginning to collapse when Paul drove wildly back down the drive — and straight into the blazing doors of the building. The workshop fell around him in a great roaring cloud of sparks and flame. There was a brief extra burst of flame when the petrol in the tank of the car exploded.

"He was mad all right," said Harry to Paul's wife in bed a couple of nights later. "We could hear him shouting as he drove past us, just before he crashed into the workshop."

EIGHT

SEWING-MACHINE

It was okay before they got there, but once they were standing around looking into it things were a bit different. Tony's first thought was that the thick tow-rope he'd carried up through the bush wasn't too ridiculously long and thick after all. Tom was feeling embarrassed for his brother John, who'd committed himself to going down first. John was feeling a bit embarrassed for himself too but not letting on.

"It's pretty dark in there."

"Should have brought a torch or something."

"Anyone got any matches?"

"Yes. I've got some. Here."

"You might have trouble lighting them."

"Wonder how deep it is."

"Let's throw something in."

They dropped a big lump of rotten timber down the old mineshaft. After a long time the sound of it plunging into water came up out of the black hole — *cheow cheowcheow*.

"It's pretty deep."

"It's full of water."

"Let's find another one," said Tom suddenly. "A smaller one."

"No," said John sharply. "I'm going down this one. Give me the rope."

"What about the water?"

"Who's scared of a bit of water? I'll go down as far as the water and have a look around and then come up again.

Give me the matches."

They made a loop in one end of the rope for John to stand in and tied the other end to a small tree near the shaft. Then he took off his gumboots and they lowered him slowly down into the hole. It was a long time before he was out of sight. They shouted quickly back and forth in and out of the darkness.

"Are you all right?"

"I can see the moon up in the sky."

"Is there enough rope?"

"How the hell do I know?"

"There's not much left up here."

"Hold me there. I'll light a match."

Tony stopped feeding the loop of rope round the tree and tied it there. Looking down they saw the faint flare as John lit a match. It only lasted for a second. Then another.

"Matches won't burn. Must be something in the air down here."

"Come up again," yelled Tom. "There might be poisonous gas down there."

"Let me down a bit further," called John, "then I'll come up."

There was only a few feet of the rope left and Tom and Tony let it all out quickly so they could pull John up again, out of this stupid hole.

"That's all the rope," Tom yelled into the hole.

John's voice sounded small and strange coming in faint echoes up the shaft. "I'll try the matches again."

This time they could see no flare at all.

"No good. I've dropped the matches now anyway."

"Come up," yelled Tom. "Come on, Tony. We'll start pulling him up. He's been down there long enough."

"Wait on," said Tony. "He's saying something."

"What's that?" called Tom down the shaft.

John's voice floated raggedly up to them with a faint trace of panic in it. "You'd better pull me up. The rope's cutting my feet."

"Quick, pull him up," said Tom. "Pull him up!"

They grabbed the rope and pulled.

"Hell, he's heavy," said Tony.

"Keep pulling."

"Listen. He's saying something."

"Keep pulling," said Tom. "Harder!"

"I can't. Let's have a spell."

"No. Keep pulling."

"It's no good. I can't hold it. Let's have a spell."

"Keep pulling or I'll bash you."

"I can't."

They'd gained only a few feet and it was obvious that they weren't going to be able to hold him.

"Tie the rope round the tree. Tie the rope round the tree. *Tie the rope round the tree!*"

John was shouting something down in the mineshaft but they couldn't hear. When Tony let go the rope to make a hitch round the tree Tom couldn't take the weight. He was dragged to the edge of the hole and the rope slipped faster and faster through his burning hands until it stopped with a jerk. Tom leaned gasping over the edge. John's voice came weakly up to him. Tony stood white by the tree.

"Tom. Tom. Get me out. I can't hold on."

"Wait on. We'll pull you up in a minute."

"No, now. I can't hold on. The rope keeps turning round all the time. My feet are hurting."

Tom could scarcely hear what he was saying. It sounded as if he was coughing or sobbing. Tom jumped to his feet and grabbed the rope again, shouting to Tony to pull. But it was no use. They got a few feet of rope in the first frantic burst of energy and then it just slipped away from them again.

"You'll have to go and get someone," said Tom to Tony. "Hurry up. Run!"

"Who shall I get?"

"Anyone," said Tom savagely. "Stop a car down on the road. Go on."

Tony ran off down the bush track. There were noises down in the mine. Tom crawled over to the edge and looked down the rope to where it disappeared.

"What's happening? What are you doing?" called John in a funny voice.

"Tony's gone for help. Just hang on for a little while. They'll be here in a minute."

"I can't. I can't hold on any longer. My feet are hurting. My hands — do something."

"Hold on. Save your breath and hold on!"

There was a silence, worse than John's unfamiliar distorted voice from the black throat of the mine. Then he called again, strangely calm now. He wasn't shouting but Tom could hear what he was saying more distinctly.

"Tom. Are you there, Tom?"

"Yes, I'm here. It won't be long now."

"Tom?"

"What?"

"Tom, I'm sorry about the bike. It wasn't your fault."

"That's nothing. Don't worry about it."

Tom felt annoyed with himself for being annoyed with John

67

for talking such rubbish. It scared him.

"Tom, tell Mum it was me who broke the sewing machine. Tell her, Tom."

"Ar, don't be silly." Tom was really frightened now.

"Hold on. They're coming."

"Tom!"

"What?"

"Promise to tell Mum it was me who broke the sewing-machine. Tell her, Tom. Tell her it was . . ."

"Yes, yes. Hold on."

"No. I can't. My feet are hurting. My hands . . ."

"Hold on. Hold on!" shouted Tom desperately.

There was a horrible sound down in the hole. Like a broken scream that had already fallen into the rocks and slime down there. It struck Tom numb and cold.

"No. No." He grabbed the rope and shook it savagely. It hung loose and slack. John had fallen into the echoing depths of the black watery earth. Tom began to be sick into the grass in great gulping sobs. Voices sounded in the bush behind him but it didn't matter any more. John was dead.

When the rope dragged itself out of his cramped hands John heard himself shout or scream something. And then there was a thudding splash and he was suddenly sitting in six inches of rotten leaves and water.

He began to laugh and then it turned into crying and then back to laughter. Twenty feet above him four heads against the sky began to shout questions and instructions. The loop of the rope dangled in his face.

He was going to be in for it if he couldn't bribe young Tommy not to tell on him about breaking Mum's sewing-machine.

NINE
TAXI

The first person Jeremy Cosgrove asked next morning, the waitress who brought him his breakfast, told him how to find Mrs Mobberley.

"Well, you go out past the cemetery and turn left just before you get to Millers'. Mobberleys' is the last place on the right past Bluskers' before you get to where the Driddles used to live before they shifted into their new place next to Cross's."

Cosgrove thanked her and went out on to the street to look for a taxi. He found it parked outside Ongapuni's one garage, and then he was sent, twice, from one end of the town and back again by people who didn't like to admit that they didn't know where the taxi-driver was to be found. He eventually traced that gentleman to the public bar of the hotel, where he'd come from in the first place almost an hour before.

Cosgrove had never been able to appreciate the languorous mental and physical attitudes of these country folk, though he always managed to keep his irritation private. But when he was bumbled around by them like this he often became very agitated, and he didn't like being agitated because he could never safely express his agitation for fear of copping a smack in the kisser. It was very frustrating.

And after an hour of the mounting tension involved in something so simple as finding the local taxi-driver, the taxi-driver himself proved uncooperative. Cosgrove asked the publican if he would mind pointing out which was the taxi-driver, and the publican, whose both hands were occupied with something in his pockets, nodded his head wisely in the general direction of two men deep in urgent conversation at the far end of the bar.

As he approached these two men Cosgrove saw that they were both so un-taxi-driverish-looking that he was tempted to suspect the publican of having played some kind of joke on him. And when he was close enough to address them they went on talking as though he was invisible.

"Well, as I said at the time, Bert, there's no tellin' how many's goin' t' turn up, and that's a fact."

"Yeah, there's no tellin' how many of 'em's goin' t' turn up alright. I backed yerrup on that, remember?"

"I think I did 'ear somethin', Bert. But it was me told 'em t' git another twenty tickets extra, above and beyond what they reckoned they was goin' t' need."

"Yeah, well I mentioned it t' Stew Miller when we first went in the first place and he said f' me t' bring it up after the meetin' but you got in first. Stew'll tell y'. You arst 'im if I come up to 'im when we first went in. . . ."

"Excuse me," said Cosgrove politely. "Is one of you gentlemen the taxi-driver?"

For a moment it didn't look as though either of them were going to answer him. They didn't turn their heads to look at him, as he had every right to expect them to; they turned their whole bodies, ever so slowly, until they'd about-faced and were leaning with their drinks in their hands and their backs against the bar, looking at him.

For a long time they stood like that and then Cosgrove saw that one of them was actually going to speak. He saw the

70

decision on the face, the bracing of the lungs, the intake of breath, the pause, the mouth beginning to open. . . .

"Yeah. That's right," he drawled.

It took Cosgrove a moment to remember the question and then relate it to the answer. Then he addressed himself to the talkative one.

"I was wondering if you could run me out to where Mrs Mobberley lives?"

The taxi-driver thought it over for a few seconds.

"Not me, mate," he said. "I'd like to be able to help y', but I can't. Haven't got a car or anythin'."

Another pause, this time from Cosgrove.

"Is your taxi not working at the moment?" he enquired.

" 'S'not *my* taxi, mate, it's me mate 'ere's."

Cosgrove felt his temper begin to rise alarmingly and then slowly subside as he deftly reduced the consequences of saying what he felt to its lowest probable common denominator — a belt in the ear from both sides at once. He turned to the other man, who looked even less like a taxi-driver than the other had.

"Could *you* drive me out to Mrs Mobberley's place?" he asked through politely clenched manners.

The second taxi-driver thoughtfully considered the proposition for a few moments. Cosgrove's thumb went through the lining of his pocket with a loud *brip* that caused both taxi-drivers to deepen their looks at him warily. At last the second taxi-driver spoke.

"I spose so," he grunted. "Don't see why not." He turned to his mate for approval of the decision.

"Sure, don't see why not," his mate agreed.

"Thank you," said Cosgrove, turning to lead the way

out to the footpath.

"I'm going right past Missus Mobberley's place this afternoon," went on the real taxi-driver. "I could drop you off on the way if you like," he added generously.

Cosgrove, frozen in his half-turned-away position, felt all his pores open and close like anemones. "I'd really prefer to go now, if you could manage it," he said. "I'm in a rather urgent hurry as a matter of fact. I only have a few hours to get a lot of work done. I have to meet a deadline."

"In a hurry, eh?"

"Yes, I *am* in a hurry."

"Well if you're in a hurry I might be able to help you out." He drank from his glass.

"That's very kind of you," said Cosgrove, prepared to think a little more kindly of the man, now that he had things moving.

"She's right, mate . . ." He paused as though he'd just made a curious discovery. ". . . You're new around here, aren't you?"

"Yes. Look, could we go now please? I am in a hurry. It's urgent."

"In that case I don't see why we shouldn't get away right now," said the taxi-driver actively.

"Well let's get along, shall we?" urged Cosgrove.

The taxi-driver drained his glass and put it on the bar. "Don't fill that one up again, Bert," he instructed. "I've got to dash now. Got to get this bloke over to Missus Mobberley's. He's in a hurry."

"Okay then," replied Bert understandingly. "See y' when y' git back."

"Righto, see you when I get back. . . . Will y' be in 'ere?"

"Think so. Either in 'ere or over Bill's place."

"Okay. If y' not in 'ere I'll 'ave a look over at Bill's place."

Cosgrove was following the taxi-driver out the door when Bert spoke from behind them at the bar. The taxi-driver stopped and Cosgrove cannoned into him.

"I'll most likely be in 'ere," Bert had said.

"Okay," said the taxi-driver. "I'll look in 'ere first."

"Righto."

"See y'."

And suddenly Cosgrove and his captive taxi-driver were out on the footpath, actually moving towards the taxi, which was parked about 150 yards from the hotel.

"Are you very busy at the moment?" he enquired pleasantly, to dispel the odd feeling that it had all been too easy and something would yet intervene to prevent him from getting to Mrs Mobberley.

"Comes and goes," replied the taxi-driver. "As a matter of fact," he confided, "I don't know too much about the taxi business. I just took over the outfit."

"Is that a fact?" said Cosgrove uneasily.

"Yeah, bought Ronnie Wall out. Matter of fact I been a farmer all me life. The doc made me sell out the farm and take on a lighter caper because of me 'ealth."

"Really?"

"Yeah. Got a crook ticker on me. Coronary Thrombosis."

"I'm very sorry to hear it," said Cosgrove absently, reaching to open the front passenger's door of the taxi.

"Yeah," agreed the taxi-driver sympathetically. "It's a bit of a blow to a man all right, havin' to' take it easy after workin' 'ard all me life."

Cosgrove had got into the taxi and closed the door, so the

taxi-driver went round to his side and opened that door and began to climb in.

"Still it's no good complainin'," he went on. "Worries the missus more than me." He slammed the door. "Yeah, when a man's time's up he's a gonner, I reckon. No use worryin' about it."

Cosgrove watched in rising apprehension as the taxi-driver fumbled at his pocket openings. He sat there in silence for a moment and then he said: "I'm gunner have t' get out again. I've forgot to take me keys out of me pocket before I got in. Always doin' that. Funny, isn't it?"

Cosgrove didn't think it was funny enough to be worth the strain of making a polite comment. The taxi-driver got out and plunged his hands into his cluttered pockets several times each. "I'm a beaut at losin' things," he announced with a bashful grin.

This was the final straw. Cosgrove felt his willpower begin to smoulder restlessly inside him. If the taxi-driver announced the loss of his ignition key Cosgrove wasn't going to be responsible for his words or actions. He half closed his eyes and waited fearfully for the terrible pronouncement.

"Ah," said the taxi-driver. "Got 'em. Knew all along they was in me pocket somewhere."

Cosgrove relaxed. Then the taxi-driver bent down to look into the car.

"Just hold the fort 'ere for a mo, will y' mate?" he said. "Just remembered somethin'. Won't be a tick."

Cosgrove nodded dumbly. The taxi-driver began to cross the street and stopped to look both ways for traffic on the silent thoroughfare, then moved towards the other side. Out of the corner of his eye Cosgrove saw him pause, think, and slowly retrace his steps. He came and opened the door of the cab and looked in again.

"Anything y' want from the shop, mate?" he asked.

"Nup," was all Cosgrove could say to thank him for his thoughtfulness.

"Okay. Just thought if there was something y' wanted I could have picked it up f' y', seein' as I'm goin' along there meself."

As Cosgrove couldn't answer he closed the door, looked both empty ways again, crossed the road, and ambled slowly out of sight along the footpath.

When his driver had gone Cosgrove sighed loudly several times in the hot cab and wondered if he wished he were back in the office. He couldn't decide, so he wondered about Mrs Mobberley. From a dozen cross-pollinations of the stock that bred men such as the taxi driver, Mrs Mobberley would have sprouted, flowered briefly, and then married back into. Cosgrove had known exactly what kind of woman she was as soon as he'd heard about her. He'd met them in dozens of country places, just like this one. Even the same smells and times of year. He'd met them in hundreds of different interviews in thousands of different shapes and dresses and faces and circumstances. This sounded like a great variety, and it was. In fact Cosgrove had decided that they lacked variety in only two respects: they were all colourless, and all ignorant. What other kind of woman would fit into the environs of the country's stately cow sheds and woolsheds?

And her husband would come in from his labours and hover within earshot, on hand to see that nothing bad for the family got into the papers. ("I knocked off and went up to the house when that reporter bloke came to see the missus the other day, Jim. You can't trust them bastards as far as you can kick 'em. They put words in your mouth, that's what they do. If he'd tried any of his funny stuff with my missus he'd have been out the gate quicker than he came in, I can tell you!")

After all, Cosgrove reflected, you can't blame these men. Mrs Mobberley had only done what is expected of the wives of men of this calibre. No strangers to violence, these sturdy fellows. (One of them once punched Cosgrove in the face and split his lip because the typesetter on another paper had got his name wrong in a list of people convicted and fined for after-hours drinking.) Such a man would have handled Mrs Mobberley's story without any of this newspaper nonsense. He would have simply walked on up, drawn back his powerful right arm, and pulled out his holstered tobacco in one smooth movement.

Cosgrove was so engrossed in taking out his frustrations on these absent members of the taxi-driver's kin that he failed to hear him returning. The sudden rattle of the opening door started Cosgrove's visions into guilty cover.

"Forgot me smokes," said the taxi-driver gravely, settling into his seat and fumbling patiently on the wrong end of a new packet of cigarettes for the cellophane tag opener. "I'm no good without me smokes."

He got the packet open and broke the ends of two cigarettes with his clumsy fingers before he succeeded in extracting one. Then he patted his pockets and gazed blankly around the silent cab. Cosgrove waited for it with the teeth on the blind side of his face gritted and the lips on the taxi-driver's side hooked back into the best he could do in the way of a smile. Then the taxi-driver turned to him and spoke with all the exasperation of someone whose just been robbed.

"I don't suppose you've got a match on you by any chance, mate?"

"I'm sorry," said Cosgrove. "I don't smoke."

"Strike," said the taxi-driver. "I forgot to offer you one. Here, help yourself."

"I don't smoke," repeated Cosgrove.

"She's right," said the taxi-driver reassuringly. "I've got plenty."

"I don't smoke."

"Take one for later then," said the taxi-driver encouragingly.

"I don't smoke."

"Don't smoke, eh?" said the taxi-driver. His tone suggested that he was quite prepared to believe Cosgrove didn't smoke, but he found it difficult.

"Couldn't do without me smokes meself. Not that I hold it against a joker that doesn't smoke. If they don't want to smoke that's their business. I don't believe in interferin' in anyone's private affairs. . . ."

He broke off to reach over and rummage in the glovebox in front of Cosgrove. "Did you see where I put me matches?" he asked.

"No, as a matter of fact I didn't," said Cosgrove, leaning back into the seat out of the way of the taxi driver's rummaging.

"I bet that bloody Bert's got them, that's what'll have happened. Bert's lifted 'em. He's a beaut at that caper."

Cosgrove could see a box of matches between some papers in the glovebox and was about to say so when the taxi-driver found another box, all on his own.

"There y'are," he said triumphantly. I knew I had a box of matches in there somewhere." He lit his cigarette. "Sure you won't have one?" he enquired.

"Quite sure, thank you," said Cosgrove firmly.

"Well, I'll just leave 'em on the seat 'ere so you can bog into 'em if you change your mind later on."

As far as Cosgrove could see there was now no reason why they couldn't set off. He waited to see what would happen.

The taxi-driver must have had similar thoughts. "Well, we could get away now," he said. "Don't want to hold you up if you're in a hurry."

He fumbled at himself for a few moments.

"Looks like I'm goin t' have to get out again," he said resignedly. "I've gone and forgotten to get me keys out of me pants pocket again. Don't seem to 'ave been doin' anything but get in and out of the bloody car all day. It's tough on a man with a crook ticker, y'know." He held up the found keys. "Knew they were there somewhere," he grinned, getting back into the car and slamming the door.

He put the key in the ignition switch, turned it on and pressed the starter. Incredibly, the car started. And then, even more incredibly, they moved off along the road with a series of gentle jerks.

Cosgrove felt an absurd desire to apologise to the taxi-driver for his lack of faith in him. Instead he asked: "Is it very far to Mrs Mobberley's place?"

"No distance at all, mate. No distance at all. Just out this way a bit."

The vehicle accelerated violently and Cosgrove thought with a slash of panic of the taxi-driver's Coronary Thrombosis. He flung a look at the speedometer. They were travelling at fifteen miles an hour in second gear and had covered just under one hundred yards.

A hundred and thirty yards from the last of Ongapuni's shops (Cosgrove idly paced out these distances on a walk later) the taxi rolled gently around a left-hand turn at an elegant five miles an hour, off the town's bitumen strip and on to a long straight metalled road.

"Don't like goin' too fast just yet," explained the taxi-driver. "Pays to take it easy at first."

"Do you mean you're only learning to drive a car?" demanded Cosgrove, his voice harsh with alarm.

"Been at it close on three weeks now," said the taxi-driver proudly. "Speed's the thing causes all the accidents, y'know. I'm not goin' to do any speedin' till I get used to it."

"You mean you don't even hold a taxi licence?"

"Nar, the traffic bloke only comes out 'ere every four months or so," explained the taxi-driver. "If I can catch 'im next time he comes I'll hit 'im for a licence."

"I certainly hope you do," said Cosgrove, and he couldn't help adding: "But you'll probably have to *hold* him up for it, by the look of things."

The taxi-driver let the car drift to a stop in the centre of the road. Cosgrove mistook the grim look of concentration on his face for anger at his sarcastic remark. He hadn't realised that the man was so sensitive.

"Look, I'm terribly sorry," he blurted. "I had no intention of offending you. I had no idea . . ." He saw by the way the taxi-driver was looking at him that something was wrong. "What's wrong?" he asked, clearing his throat to cover up the quavering in his voice.

"There's nothing wrong with me, mate," said the taxi-driver.

"Then why have we stopped here like this?"

"This is where you wanted to go, isn't it? Mrs Mobberley's place?"

"Yes, Mrs Mobberley's place. I want to interview her."

"Well, you're there, mate. That's her house in behind them trees there."

Cosgrove got woodenly out of the car and looked back up the road. There was the main road they'd turned off a few moments ago, still there. (Two hundred and ten yards). And there was the town. Ongapuni, less than a quarter of a mile across the paddocks, two or three hundred yards, a few minutes' walk. And there was the letterbox, MOBBERLEY painted on it. And there in the taxi was the taxi-driver, happily puffing on that same cigarette, with all the satisfaction of having tackled a difficult job, and done it well. To him it was perfectly logical for someone to hire a taxi for a journey so short that the vehicle didn't have time to get into top gear. Cosgrove felt suddenly fond of the fumbling taxi-driver; they'd been through so much together. Incredible that it was only an hour and a half since he'd left the hotel in search of Mrs Mobberley. It seemed like weeks. It was crazy.

He walked round to the taxi-driver's open window.

"How much do I owe you?" he asked generously.

"Ar, cut it out mate. I wouldn't charge a man for a bit of a trip like that. Forget it — here, have a smoke."

He passed the opened packet out and Cosgrove took the cigarette his taxi-driver knew he needed all the time. Then Cosgrove moved towards the side of the road as the taxi-driver jerked away with a nod and a "See y' later," and drove away at a sedate few miles an hour, not back towards the town, but straight away along the middle of the road in the direction he was facing. It was a long time before he passed out of sight. To Cosgrove there was only one possible explanation. The taxi-driver had obviously decided to drive straight on, right around the world and back into Ongapuni from the other way, rather than go to all the bother of turning his taxi round. Perhaps he didn't know about the reverse gear.

Cosgrove walked up and down along the road outside the Mobberley place until he'd recovered a little from the strain of getting there. Then, almost completely restored, he walked up the path and pressed the front doorbell with all the confidence you get free with every lifetime of experience.

Nothing, after all, could be worse than what had already happened to him that morning.

TEN

HIS JUST DESERTS

(Mrs Mobberley's story as told to Jeremy Cosgrove)

Years ago, during the Depression, when I was only six years old, my father got a job as a coalminer and we went to live in a remote mining settlement on the West Coast.

The owner of the mine was a great bully of a man called Big Nudd. He was huge and powerful and had the whole district in a state of confusion and fear. He rode up and down the muddy bush roads on a big flat-decked dray which was drawn by two nervous, ill-treated horses. We soon learned that Big Nudd would give a man a job and a house to live in, and then visit his wife and family while he was down in the mine. I don't think he actually got up to any real physical mischief, but he seemed to enjoy terrorising the defenceless women and children. The approach of the big dray, rumbling along the road on its iron wheels, would send everyone scuttling apprehensively for cover inside their houses.

Many of the women were too afraid for their husbands, themselves, or just the jobs, to tell their husbands what was going on while they were underground. But such conditions cannot be kept secret for long. Husbands became suspicious. Homes broke up. Occasionally a desperate husband or father would try to fight Big Nudd, but they always ended up injured and jobless for their pains, while their wives and families would have to find somewhere to live and something to eat for themselves until they'd recovered.

For some reason Big Nudd never bothered my mother or me, and I remember Mother saying once that Father must have had some kind of arrangement with him. But my father would refuse to discuss it whenever she introduced the subject.

This was the situation in the settlement for several months after we arrived there. Father seemed content enough to simply have sufficient money coming in to keep us going until the Depression ended. None of us could afford to move on to another place, and Big Nudd, in his brutish way, took advantage of the situation at every opportunity. I think he must have enjoyed the hold he had over the people who were forced by circumstances to work for him.

Life went on in the little settlement with a strange atmosphere of waiting; waiting for some relief from the financial rigours of the Depression, from the constant striving to keep enough food in the houses to feed the people, and from the persecutions of Big Nudd. Then relief from one of these things came in a most unexpected way.

The people of the settlement had organised a dance to celebrate the wedding of a popular young man who was bringing his bride back from one of the large towns on the Coast. Straight after the service he was to put his bride on the bus and return with her to the settlement, where he had a job and a house to live in. About five miles from the village was a hall, where they were to stop off for the usual celebration. The bus would then go into the settlement to collect all those who didn't have cars and return with them to the hall. The bus would collect them from the hall at midnight and take them back to the village.

All these arrangements were made as discreetly as possible,

for fear that Big Nudd would come to hear of the function, which he would have taken great delight in crashing in on and breaking up, either by getting drunk and smashing things or by simply being there.

We drove to the hall in our car and arrived early to help with the supper and the organising of things. By the time the bus with the rest of the people arrived and had greeted and toasted the newly-weds, it was getting dark. At eight o'clock I was put to bed on the back seat of our car, wrapped warmly in blankets, as I usually was on these occasions.

I used to enjoy sleeping in the car at parties and things. I could either sit up peeping at the people and lights, or lie there listening to the singing and voices until I went to sleep. It was very exciting and my parents were always close by so I was never afraid.

On this night I knelt up in my blankets with my chin on the ledge of the car door, watching the funny shadows of the people as they passed through the band of light coming from the hall doorway, which cut across the stony area in front of the building, slicing cars and trees right in half.

It must have been about half past nine in the evening and the people were all inside the hall, dancing and laughing and drinking toasts, when Big Nudd s dray came trundling up out of the darkness, its big iron-shod wheels crackling on the stones as it passed through my patch of light, making a huge shadow across the ground and parked cars, with Big Nudd hunched like a great motionless bear with the reins slack in the lumpy silhouette of his hands. The strange contraption passed through the light and stopped with a growl on the far side. I could just see the end of the dray and one big spoked wheel at the edge of the light. I remember wondering if the horses could see me from out there in the dark if they looked.

Big Nudd scraped and creaked off the dray and clumped in his big boots into the light towards the hall doorway, almost shutting off the light completely for a moment as he passed through the door and disappeared inside. The noisy laughter stopped suddenly, and then slowly picked up again with a lower, slower sound to it.

Then I heard a voice, raised indignantly, shout, "Private function!" A roar from Big Nudd and then a bump and a shriek of screams from the women that faded quickly to indignant murmuring.

After a while the music started up again in a half-hearted kind of way, and there was nothing much to see for a long time. Once my mother came out to see if I was all right, and, as usual, I ducked into my sleeping position and pretended to be asleep. When she had gone I lay there listening. I heard some men walk out past the car towards the grass and didn't look because I was a young lady. I heard one of them say,

". . . just walked in and blew his nose on her veil."

And another said:

"There'll be trouble here tonight, you mark my words. I'm going to round up my wife and kids and get off home before he gets any more of that wine and beer under his belt."

"What about the rest of us?" asked another. "Most of us have to wait for the bus."

"Someone'll kill him one of these days," said another man.

The men then went back into the hall, taking their voices with them.

I slept a little after that and only half-woke every now and again when an uproar started in the hall, or when my mother or father came out to see if I was all right. Then I heard something I didn't recognise, but it woke me instantly. I rose up to peek carefully over the car door.

The hunched figure of Big Nudd wavered drunkenly along the wall to one side of the hall doorway, his monstrous black shadow sliding back and forth in and out of the darkness. As I watched he took a jerky step forward and put one arm out to lean on the wall. Then he turned towards me and raised one hand to wipe his mouth as though he was going to eat it like a big toffee apple. He began to stumble and grope his way towards the car, grunting and spitting.

I was terrified, but I kept watching as he came right up to the car. Just as he was about to crash the whole car, with me in it, to pieces, he veered past. I heard the faint rasp of his hand on the bodywork and felt the car sway ever so slightly as he leaned on it in passing. The sound of his boots, scuffling erratically on the gravel, stopped, and then scuffled on into the darkness.

Suddenly I heard the raised voice of my mother and saw the people crowded silently in the doorway of the hall. This silence was what had awakened me. There was a slight commotion as my mother was bustled protesting into the hall, attended by several comforting women.

Big Nudd appeared, stumbling weakly along at the edge of the light towards the dray. He found it and crawled on to the tray, for all the world like a big pup trying to climb steps. He crawled along the dray until only his legs and one arm could be seen in the light. Then he lay still and in a few seconds he began to snore huge snores.

Somebody at the hall doorway said in a loud voice:

"It's all right now, he's out cold. I've seen him like this before. He won't wake up for hours."

"Not surprising, with all he's drunk. It's a wonder he doesn't kill himself," said someone else.

"It's a *pity* he doesn't kill himself," said a woman.

"Okay now, back to the party everybody," called somebody importantly.

And people began to drift back into the hall. My mother and father both hurried out towards the car and I ducked quickly under my blankets and went to sleep while my mother tucked me in and shushed my father not to make a noise and wake me. When they went back into the hall I sat up and kneeled, looking at Big Nudd's half-lit shape lying out there on the cold hard dray.

It seemed like hours that I sat there, staring at him, watching the light ebb and flow across a square bulge in his hip pocket as he breathed his great beery snores. The noise inside the hall rose up in laughter and shouts and the thumping rhythm of accordion and piano. There was a lot of drinking, I could tell by the sound of the bursts of laughter that poured from the hall every now and then. Big Nudd could hear none of this.

Suddenly there was a figure standing in the dark beside Big Nudd's dray. In the shadows just beyond the light a shoulder, half-lit. I thought Big Nudd was going to be robbed, but the shadowy figure began to struggle with his shoulders, as though he was going to wake him and invite him into the warm hall before he caught cold. The strange tussle went on for some time, and then there was a slight thump and a halting snort in Big Nudd's snoring, and suddenly his face appeared upside down, framed in the light between two of the big wheel-spokes.

I was first surprised and then frightened as the figure in the darkness bent forward momentarily into the light. It was my father.

I must admit that I was only frightened to see one of my own parents so close to someone like Big Nudd, whom everybody was so afraid of. My father withdrew into the darkness and even the glow of his white shirt was no longer visible. Only Big Nudd's huge face, illuminated between the spokes.

I remember wondering why my father had bothered to touch him in that strange way, and how he could be lying with his face upside down like that with his jaw hanging open upwards. In fact I lay back across the car seat to try it for myself.

When I looked back towards the dray where these strange things had taken place, I heard the shuffle and creak of Big Nudd's horses beyond the light in the darkness. Suddenly a horse snickered and shuddered in its harness, with several quick nervous stamps of hooves, and Big Nudd's face was suddenly snatched out of sight and carried away on a plunging rattle of sound that receded into the cold blackness of the night, along a rough mill-road that joined the main road at the hall and had fallen into disuse since the Depression had closed the mill.

Although my memory of all this is very clear, I did not then realise the implications of what I had witnessed. The sounds of Big Nudd's dray had scarcely rumbled away into silence when I saw a figure, my father, move mothlike through the light from a window down the side of the hall towards the rear door.

After what seemed a long time, a man came out of the hall, looked around, and then began to move back inside.

"I thought I heard a noise out here," he said to someone just inside the door.

"I'm sure I did," said the other man, pushing past him.

Suddenly there were people everywhere, milling in the light and demanding to know what was going on.

"It sounded like horses," said a lady.

"Hey! Big Nudd's wagon has gone," called a man from over where it had been.

"His horses must have bolted with him. He was in no condition to drive them away."

"Is that kid all right?" asked my father, pushing his way through the crowd towards the car.

I got quickly into my sleeping position and lay listening, and wondering.

"She's okay," said a voice near the car. But my father and mother both came to make sure.

"Better make certain that Big Nudd's not hanging around somewhere," warned a voice. "He'll be in an ugly mood by now if he is."

"He might have woken up and just gone off home," suggested my mother, moving away from the car.

"What about all that noise we heard? It sounded as though his wagon was out of control."

"We'd better have a look," said one of the main men. "He was pretty drunk, and those horses of his are skittery enough to have bolted with him."

Nobody was very concerned about Big Nudd really, and nobody could blame them, but they brought lights and some of the men moved off to look for him, reluctant to bother but brave in a group. I sat up as my mother opened the door of the car and told me we were leaving. My father said goodbyes to some friends who had to wait for the bus at midnight, and we drove away, leaving people standing in little groups outside the hall, with glowing cigarettes and getting ready to leave.

We weren't even there when they brought Big Nudd's almost headless body in and laid it in a corner of the hall under a blanket. And nobody ever asked me if I'd heard or seen anything. Never a whisper of suspicion about the way Big Nudd died. It was put down to a simple accident and forgotten about as quickly as possible in the relief everybody felt at his passing. As far as most of them were concerned it was a matter of his having received his just deserts.

ELEVEN

A Clean Swap

Midday and steaming hot. The gentle *kiukiuing* of pigeons in the teatrees. Hushing of air through she-oaks and rifle-fish splashing in the shade under banks. Leaves and debris on the smooth water revolving slowly upstream on a filling tide, and around the bend the coming and going stink of something rotten a crocodile had hidden somewhere.

The twenty-five-foot canoe they'd bought off the blacks down the river for a sack of flour and a packet of Log Cabin tobacco moved sullenly upstream with the current under their lazy paddling. Over the heap of supplies and gear on the platform in the centre of the canoe Ralph could see by the movement of Bill's shoulder muscles that he wasn't putting any weight into the paddle. It didn't matter much. There was no hurry, and Bill would be doing most of the paddling tonight.

One thing about these canoes, they were so big and heavy that once you got them moving they carried along without much effort to the paddlers. Another thing about them was that once you got them moving they took a hell of a lot of stopping or manoeuvring. They missed out on a lot of crocs that way.

If they'd kept off the grog in Normanton that last skin cheque would have bought them an outboard motor. Oh well — next time perhaps.

Bill in the bow stopped pretending to paddle and turned round in his seat.

"Smell that?" he asked.

"Yeah." Ralph paddled slowly on. "Croc?"

"Could be."

"How much further do we have to go before we can camp?" asked Bill, laying his paddle across the canoe and getting his tobacco out of the hip pocket of his shorts.

"We'll keep going till the tide turns," said Ralph, who was the unofficial head man because of having been at the game for three years. "They don't like you camping too close to the mission and we don't want to louse things up here. We won't get supplies anywhere else."

"What's wrong with camping near the mission?" Bill wanted to know.

Ralph grinned. "The gins," he said. "They sneak away and get hanging around your camp."

He trailed his paddle and steered the canoe away from a petrified stump that showed a few inches under the water.

"You could always hunt them out of it," said Bill.

"You could," agreed Ralph, "but you don't. It's better to have nothing to do with them."

Bill picked up his paddle and turned back to his job. "You'd never catch me having anything to do with those scrawny bitches," he said.

"That's what everyone says," replied Ralph. "But there's still plenty of half-caste kids running around the scrub. You can't blame the mission blokes being a bit down on it."

They lapsed into silence, broken only by the plop-swirling of the paddles, until a couple of bends later Bill pointed to a wet smooth mud-slide on a sloping bank among an isolated stand of mangroves.

"Slide."

"Yeah," said Ralph interestedly. "A big one, too, by the look of it."

They steered the canoe to sweep close in to the bank there.

"Fairly big saltwater-croc," announced Ralph. "We might get a crack at him later."

They paddled on and about an hour later the current on the river was still and it was high tide. They found a landing place and nosed the canoe into the shore.

"Unload everything except the shooting gear."

On the leafy bank they made a pile of their supplies and gear and Bill lit a fire. Ralph went away with the rifle to look for meat; he saw a dingo, a king-brown snake, and three wallabies. He shot a wallaby and took the hindquarters and tail back to camp. They ate damper and steaks and put on a wallaby stew with potatoes and onions.

"How much further does this river go?" asked Bill, sipping noisily at a pannikin of weak tea.

"Far as I can remember it breaks up into a lot of smaller streams not far from here," replied Ralph. "There's a big area of swamp and mud back in there. There'd be crocs in there all right, but it's a hell of a place to get at. Lousy with sandflies and mosquitos. The tide hardly reaches up into it. There's places where you can get nearly-fresh water but you have to hunt round for it. The place changes a fair bit. Hard to say what it's like now. It's two years since me and Baldy Foster shot there. Got a few crocs though, far as I can remember."

"Where will we shoot tonight?" asked Bill, poking at the stew in the camp oven.

"I think we'll go back down on the tide and wait until dark, then shoot our way back up here with the tide again. Should work out pretty right."

"In that case we'd better get going," said Bill. "I'll check the gear."

Harpoon, .303, .22, and ammunition. Knife, spotlight and the battery out of the jeep they'd left at the mission. Gaff, axe, boiling-up gear, quart pots, and mosquito repellent. Box of spares and sacks.

"Everything's here."

"Right. Let's go."

They pushed the canoe out into the river and settled down to a long paddle back down-river.

They had to wait until two hours after dark for the tide to turn before they could set off back up the river. Sitting in the light of their little fire on the bank, Bill said: "Ralph — you know Judy."

"That little gingerheaded piece in the pub at Normanton? Sure, I know her."

"I was wondering — you, er — you took her out a couple of times," he blurted out awkwardly.

"Yeah, that's right. We went over to Croydon once or twice. What about it?"

"Well, it's just that I've been going around with her for a couple of years, and — well, I wondered if you're serious about her or anything."

"Hell, man," said Ralph goodhumouredly. "She's the only decent sort in the Gulf. Everybody knows that. She's not going to be around much longer anyway. She told me she had a job jacked up in Cairns after Christmas."

"What do you mean by decent sort?" demanded Bill hotly.

"Ar, don't get me wrong, Bill. You know how it is. I didn't

know she was going steady with you. At least, she never said anything to me about it. If I'd known you were trotting her . . ."

"It doesn't matter," said Bill sulkily. "If I'd known she was shooting through to Cairns I wouldn't have agreed to come out here with you after you and Toby split up. I only did it to make some money. I don't suppose it matters now."

"Listen," said Ralph kindly. "I don't know how it was with you and Judy, but take my advice and forget her. If she's so keen on you after a couple of years that she'll go out with anyone who asks her, then she's not worth getting yourself worked up over."

Bill said nothing and soon it was time for them to go.

Out in the stream, Ralph, in the bow of the canoe, adjusted the light strapped to his forehead and clipped the leads on to the battery behind him. The light speared out through the darkness and raked the banks on either side of the river. The canoe slid silently up the river under the deft paddles, with the light searching for the red eyes of crocodiles.

Half an hour of noiseless progress and then a glimmer of red among some reeds on a bend ahead. Ralph steered the canoe towards a six-foot freshwater-croc while Bill paddled steadily on. They got that one easily.

Then they paddled on in the dark silence towards the glowing eyes of a big croc further up the river. Ralph felt the excitement that always thrilled him when he was on to a big one. He could hear Bill's heavy jerky breathing behind him as he splashed his paddle in clumsy nervousness.

Closer — the eyes vanished. He's gone down. Keep going, he'll come up again — there he is, further on. Keep going. Closer. Deep water here, a harpoon job. Closer. Pole in one hand, steering with the paddle in the other. Here we are! Lay the paddle across the canoe. Careful not to knock on the boat. The ridged snout and the bulging neck just under the water behind the eyes. Got him!

A thrashing, splashing, churning tumult and the croc disappears, but the rope looping out over the bow of the rocking canoe tells that he's fixed on the end of the quill. Lay the pole back in the canoe and grab the knife, just in case.

The rope stops feeding out. There's still a few coils left. Ralph picked up the .303 and closed the bolt on a cartridge. A gentle tug on the rope to get his position and suddenly the rest of the rope runs out and the canoe is jerked half round.

Silence. The river is oil. Crabs crack and plop in the mangroves. Water gurgles into holes in the mud. The canoe turns slackly in the current. He's got to come up for air —

Suddenly red eyes out in the middle of the stream. The comfortable roar of the .303 and the great white belly floats in the light. Quick! Drag him in before he sinks. Loop the rope round his jaws. He's still twitching. Here, let me get at him with the axe. There, that's fixed him. Drag him to the bank and we'll try and get him into the canoe. He's at least twelve feet. Skin'll be worth fifty bucks easy, if it's first grade.

With the croc lying in the canoe between them, Ralph turned off the light and they each rolled a smoke.

"A pretty good start," said Ralph, more nonchalantly than he felt.

"How many more do you think we'll get?"

"Hard to say," replied Ralph. "If we don't get any more tonight we still haven't done too bad. You can sometimes paddle all night around here and not even see one."

They drifted up to another small croc and Ralph shot it with the .22, grabbed it by the snout, chopped it behind the head with the axe and threw it into the canoe. A five-footer.

They lit up another big salty but couldn't get near him, and eventually gave him up and carried on. They got another freshy, about six feet, that didn't give them any trouble, and just before the camp they fluked an eight-foot salty asleep on the bank. Four crocs was a pretty good night's shooting in that area. They threw them into the shallow water by the camp, had a brew of tea by the light of the fire, and turned in at four o'clock.

They woke late in the morning and would have been bad-tempered if they hadn't had such a good night's shooting.

They ate wallaby stew and began skinning. The big crocs took them over an hour to skin, knifing the hide carefully off every inch of the way. It was mid-after noon by the time they had the four hides scraped, salted, and rolled up in a sack.

"About a hundred bucks' worth," announced Ralph, straightening stiffly from dumping the sack in the shade. "Tonight we'll do from here up the river. It shouldn't be such a drag as last night. Then tomorrow we can shift camp further upstream. Should be able to cover all that water in about a week. Then we'll give the whole river another rakeover down to the mission."

"When are we going back to Normanton?" asked Bill.

"Hell, man," laughed Ralph. "You still thinking about that redhead? We've only been out three weeks. We should have time to do the Roper and the Limmin before the Wet starts. We'll send away what skins we've got from the mission and take the rest back to town when we go for Christmas. We ought to have a few hundred bucks each by then."

"It's all very well for you," said Bill, "but you haven't got a woman to think of."

Ralph looked at him for a moment. "Neither have you, Bill. I told you before."

"Ar, go to hell." Bill turned away and began poking at the fire.

"Look, what's eating you?" asked Ralph reasonably.

"You know bloody well," exploded Bill, turning on him. "You ask Judy to marry you and then turn round and tell me she's no good."

"Where the hell did you get that from?" asked Ralph.

"She told me herself," said Bill belligerently.

"Well in that case why did you come out here with me in the first place?" asked Ralph, frowning.

"She only told me the night before we left," said Bill, "and I thought . . ."

"Look," interrupted Ralph. "I never did and never would ask Judy to marry me. I don't know what line of bull she's been feeding you, but it looks to me as though she's just trying to stir up trouble. Probably trying to get rid of you the easy way; by making you jealous. For God's sake forget her. She's no good to you, me, or anyone else."

"You mean you didn't tell her you'd marry her when you got back from this trip?" asked Bill doubtfully.

"Of course not," laughed Ralph, slapping him on the back. "If I was the marrying kind I'd have taken the plunge years ago. And it wouldn't have been anyone like Judy, I can tell you. Now cheer up and think about all the money we're going to make."

Bill half-grinned ruefully.

"I suppose a man's a bit of a mug at that," he muttered.

They got a fifteen-footer up the river and a couple of freshies on the way back. They shifted camp and shot five more salties in a side-arm of the river. They got a nine-footer out on the bank in broad daylight and an eight-foot freshy on a log near the new camp. They lost a big salty that nearly tipped the canoe over, and harpooned a one-eyed rogue croc in a swamp. They hacked a path for the canoe through miles of overhanging mangrove into a big stretch of open water, where they got a clear hundred and fifty dollars' worth of skins in two nights.

They were nearly out of salt, and Ralph said they wouldn't have time to hunt any more rivers before the Wet, by the time they finished this one.

In spite of all the success they were having, Bill became more and more withdrawn and brooding. He'd often go a whole day without offering a single unsolicited remark. Ralph appeared not to notice, though he knew well enough what the trouble was.

They hacked and dragged the canoe right up into a great spreading area of mud and mangroves at the head of the last creek running into the head of the river, with the intention of shooting their way back to their camp after dark. Even though it was broad daylight the air was so thick with mosquitos that the place droned with them.

"Well," said Ralph, spreading another dose of Kokoda round his neck. "This is as far as we go."

"Yeah," said Bill, slapping at his bare legs.

"Paddle us across to that little island there, Bill. I'll see if I can get a fire going to keep these mossies away. It's still a couple of hours or so till dark. They'll eat us alive by then. A man wouldn't survive a night in this place without a fire."

He stepped ashore and began scouting around for firewood, leaving Bill to hold the canoe against the bank.

"There's a bit of wood in here," he called. "Tie the canoe up, Bill, and come and give us a hand to rake a fire together. It's

101

pretty scattered. And bring the matches with you."

There was no answer.

"Hey, Bill," he called. "Where the hell are you?"

Still no answer. Ralph went to the edge of the mangroves and looked out. Bill was paddling quickly back down the creek.

"Hey, Bill," he yelled. "Where are you going? Come back here. Hey Bill — Bill!"

But Bill paddled round the bend out of sight without looking back.

Ralph stumbled and scrambled through the tangled masses of mangrove roots to the end of the little island. And then he stopped. There was fifty yards of muddy water between him and the main bank of the creek. And then miles of mangroves. Pursuit was impossible and survival in this place was only a matter of time, not counting the likelihood of his being taken by a crocodile on the swim from the island to the creek-bank.

Already, as the repellent wore off, his bare arms and legs were black with mosquitos, and the smaller, more vicious, sandflies. In a grey cloud of insects he waded through the muddy water and began to swim quietly for the far bank.

A great, grey crocodile that had been watching, motionless, from under an uprooted tree since the canoe first arrived, lunged noiselessly into the water.

Four days later, in the early afternoon. Bill reached the mission. He tied the loaded canoe to a stake among several other canoes, climbed the bank and made his way among the huts and staring blacks to the missionary's house on a low hill a little distance away. The missionary greeted him at the gate. Bill had

his story ready, but the missionary got in first, which, in a way, was just as well for Bill.

"Your friend said you'd probably be in today or tomorrow," he said.

"Uh — what?"

"Ralph, your mate. He came in the day before yesterday with some of my boys who were out getting beef to salt down for the Wet. He'd been badly bitten by mosquitos, you know. After he left you he lost his way in a mangrove swamp and was hours getting through to open country. It's lucky my boys found him. Terrible mess he was in; mud from head to foot and very weak from mosquito bites and exhaustion."

"Yeah. Er — hard luck," gulped Bill uncomfortably. "Er — where is he now?"

"Oh, he left this morning for Normanton," said the missionary. "I lent him a battery for his jeep. He explained how you were staying on here for the wet season."

"The wet season!" said Bill. "Isn't there any way I can get out of here?"

"Not now," said the missionary. "The last supply truck went back a week ago. There'll be no transport through here until the end of March now. However, we'll be pleased to have you here for the Wet. There's such a lot to be done, we can always use an extra willing man. — Oh yes, and Ralph left a message for you. He said not to worry about his share of the skins. He's making a clean swap for something of yours in Normanton. He said you'd know what he meant."

TWELVE

WHARF-AND-RAIL

Things are tough" said the stranger. "There's about a hundred blokes lined up for every job that's going. And there's nothing in my line at all."

"What do you do?" asked Kersey.

"Truck-driver. Been at it all me life. I've driven just about everything from flat-tops to logging artics, but I chucked the big stuff in years ago. I'm strictly a wharf-and-rail man now. You know, general deliveries and stuff. Wharf-and-rail's the caper. You've got to know what you're doing on wharf-and-rail."

"I'll bet," agreed Kersey. "How long since you worked?"

"About five weeks. I was driving for a crowd down south. Wharf-and-rail stuff."

"They put you off, did they?"

"No, as a matter of fact I threw it in."

"Eh?"

"I chucked it in, mate. Had to, more or less."

"How come?"

"Well, there were four of us driving for the same outfit, and one of us was going to get the push, we knew that. But what got my pricker up was when I twigged that someone was trying to put the skids under me."

"Yeah?"

"Yeah. One of the other blokes was dobbing me in to the boss. Shelfing me over all sorts of little odd things that only one of us drivers could have known about. Things like filling in all the dockets at lunchtime instead of after each delivery or pick-up. I tell you, the boss was starting to get it in for me, and I couldn't tell which one of the blokes was putting my pot on. But it had to be one of 'em. We always joked and ribbed each other around the depot, and parked up for lunch and a bit of a yarn together every day. But one of them was a bloody topper, and I couldn't for the life of me work out who it was."

"Did you ever find out?" asked Kersey.

"Too right I did. I wasn't going to let anyone get away with that sort of caper — especially with the jobs the way they are. Things are tough, you know."

"They're tough all right," agreed Kersey. "What did you do?"

"I set a trap for whoever it was. I told one of the blokes on the quiet one morning that I'd lost a crate of cosmetics the day before and signed the delivery docket with a bit of a squiggle, so they wouldn't know where it'd gone astray. He got real insulted when I asked him not to even let on to any of the other blokes. Wanted to know what I took him for, and all that sort of thing.

"As a matter of fact it didn't look as though it was him who'd been dobbing me in, but I had to make sure. Then I got one of the other blokes to one side at lunch-time and swore him to the utmost secrecy and told him I'd backed my truck into the front of a flash car trying to get into a cart-dock the day before. It didn't do any damage to the truck, I told 'im, but I'd made a hell of a mess of the grille and one of the headlights on the car. There was no one around at the time so I took off without reporting it, but now I was a bit worried in case someone had seen it and taken my number."

"How did he take it?" asked Kersey.

"Pretty good. He sympathised with me a bit, and said I'd probably get away with it, and all that sort of thing. And when I told him to keep it under his hat he just sort of grinned and told me to cut it out. Then he tipped me off not to let on to old Pat about it because he had a sneakin' suspicion that Pat was a bit of a you-know-what. Nothing definite to go on, mind you, but he'd be very careful what he said in front of him if he was me all the same.

"Well, this Pat was the other driver, the one I hadn't spoken to yet. He used to drive the big van — and he was a hell of a good driver, too. Boy, he could really handle the thing. Ugly thing to drive, it was, too, but old Pat could sling it in and out of cart-docks and traffic and little lanes and alleyways like nobody's business. The kind of bloke who roars right up to an intersection as if he hasn't seen it and then suddenly slams on the anchors just in time. Chocker-block with confidence and never made a blue. Back the thing straight into places where I'd have to take a couple of cuts with the flat-top. Finish his deliveries away ahead of anyone else and then offer to give you a hand with yours. Couldn't stand the sight of the bastard. All the same, it was hard to see him as a crawler. But it had to be one of them, so I caught him on his own when we were putting the trucks away that night. He had a swept-up sort of a Ford Consul, so I sidled up to him and sort of hinted that the best way to fiddle a bit of buckshee gas was to write in about half a gallon less than you actually put in your truck when you gassed up every morning. That way it looks as though your truck's hogging the gas a bit, but nothing to cause any suspicions. And at the end of the week you can nick away somewhere on the quiet and siphon off three or four gallons for your own bomb and no one's any the wiser."

"That's a good one," said Kersey, approvingly. "What'd he do?"

"He just looked at me and said thanks all the same but as far as he was concerned it wasn't worth risking his job for, but if I was getting away with it, good on me. Then he offered to give me a lift home in his car and, you know, by the time we got there I was starting to feel a bit of a fool for suspecting him. The only thing to do now was wait and see what happened. And I didn't have very long to wait, either."

"What happened?"

"Well, I'd no sooner bowled into work next morning when they said the boss wanted to see me about something. So I went around to the bit of a place he used for an office and as soon as I saw him I knew straight away that someone had sprung one on me.

"'I've had a report that one of our trucks backed into a car the day before yesterday and didn't stop to report it,' he said to me. 'Do you know anything about it?'

"'Not me,' I told him. 'Whoever told you that must have put you crook.'

"Well, at least I knew who the bastard was who'd been trying to put the skids under me. I decided to tip the other blokes off about him. *He* wasn't going to last long, once we all knew we had a topper amongst us. But blow me down, I was loading up some stuff for the wharf just after smoko that morning (hadn't had a chance to talk to any of the blokes yet), when they rang up a message for me to drop in at the depot and see the boss again as soon as possible. And when I got there he had all the carbons of my dockets spread out on the bit of a crate he used for a desk.

"'Are all these dockets of yours in order?' he asked me.

"'Of course they are,' I told him. 'What's wrong with them?'

"'There seems to be some mix-up over a crate of cosmetics,' he said.

"I knew what crate of cosmetics he was talking about, and it had never existed. It only took a couple of minutes to establish that someone had put him crook again and he apologised for holding me up and I went on with the job."

"So two of them were putting your weights up?" said Kersey.

"No mate, the whole three of 'em," corrected the wharf-and-rail bloke. "Y'see, when I got in to the depot that night the boss asked me to bring in my petrol sheets for him to go over with me. He said it was just to get a rough idea what my truck's fuel consumption was. But there was no doubt about it — the whole bloody three of them had been trying to put me in crook with the boss. They were probably doing the same things amongst each other at the same time. I tell you, things are tough all right."

"They're tough all right," agreed Kersey. "What some blokes'll do to hang on to a job when they're scared of losing it, eh? What happened?"

"Well, I'd had a proper gutful of it by this time, so I fronted straight up to the boss and told him straight out that it looked to me like some of the other blokes might just be carrying tales to him to try and put me in a bad light because they knew one of us was going to have to be put off.

"I'd have thought that would have at least squared me off with the boss over one or two warnings he'd given me, but it didn't. It put me further up the creek than ever. He turned round and told me that all this business was taking up far too much of his valuable time, and he couldn't afford to keep on drivers who caused trouble among the men. I tried to point out that it wasn't me who'd caused the trouble, but he came back at me by saying he'd give me one last chance. And you know what?"

"No, what?" said Kersey.

"A couple of days after that I found out the boss had told one of the other blokes that I'd been in his office making wild accusations about the other drivers, and he turned straight round and told the other two."

"That's a bit tough, isn't it?" said Kersey indignantly.

"It's tough all right," agreed the wharf-and-rail bloke.

"What did you do then?"

"Well I figured that, even with jobs the way they are, it just wasn't worth it. I knew I was a goner the moment I made a blue, I could see that. So I made up my mind to get the hell out of it the next payday. That was in just over a week's time, because we were getting paid once a fortnight. I was pretty hostile about the whole thing, I can tell you, but I didn't have any thoughts of revenge or anything like that, until a few days before I was going to leave when I was sitting in my truck filling in a docket for a drum of perfume I'd just loaded, and I was just going to move out when old Pat in his big van roared up the street, stopped outside, and shot back into the same building I was in — same kind of cart-dock outfit, only he'd come in a different door further along. He hopped out and went off whistling in the lift to collect something from a warehouse on one of the floors above.

"Now when he'd backed in I'd noticed that the top of his van just fitted under the big steel roll-up doors. They hadn't been pulled right up to the top of the doorway. There was no one else around just then, so I nicked across and pulled out the pin and let the chain out a few links and then put the pin back in again. Then I went back and sat in my truck to wait for a bit of a giggle.

"Pretty soon Pat came back with a lift full of crated outboard motors. He hand-carted them into the van among a whole lot of other stuff he had for rail despatch. He still hadn't seen me parked just along the dock; wouldn't have taken much notice anyway because I was well and truly on the outer by this time. He slammed himself into the van, kicked her in the guts, and roared out of there with his usual burst of speed.

"Well, I'd been expecting a bit of a giggle but I wasn't ready for what *did* happen. The top of the van caught on the top of the doorway and the whole van tore away from the rest of the truck with a terrible crash of splintered wood and tearing metal and falling crates and cartons and bales and boxes. And Pat was right out on to the street with the cab and chassis of his van before he could stop. I heard him get out and next thing he ran into the building, pushed the lift button, and then disappeared up some stairs. He was probably going to ring up, or get somebody, or something.

"It must have been the shock of realising what a terrible amount of damage I'd caused — or maybe it was fright, I don't know — but I suddenly got the crazy idea that if only I could put the door back the way it was before I'd let it down things wouldn't be quite so disastrous. So I got out and picked my way among all the wreckage and raised the door about six inches. It was a bit buckled but it went up all right. Then I got back in my truck and by the time I drove out of there the first few people were just arriving to see what the crash had been."

"Hell," said Kersey. "You were taking a fair sort of a risk, weren't you?"

111

"I don't mind telling you, I was worried all right. I hadn't bargained for that little lot. I don't even know what made me do it in the first place."

"Did you get away with it?"

"Yes, I did. But there wasn't much satisfaction in it, even later, when they sent me round to cart away some of the undamaged stuff from Pat's van. The traffic cops were there, and quite a little crowd was watching a bunch of blokes measuring and equating and theorising and arguing and reconstructing; trying to work out how an eleven-foot van could have caught on an eleven-foot-nine doorway. They wouldn't let me touch any of the stuff until it had all been weighed, and I had to stand around and watch and listen.

"Pat was there, being questioned by two blokes who looked like they came from the insurance company. I heard one of them say, 'It's impossible, I tell you!'

"They sealed off the door the way it was and the insurance company paid a man to stand guard all night, and next day they got a van the same as Pat's from somewhere and drove it back and forth, in and out of that cart-dock, with exactly the same load and at all sorts of different speeds and angles. But no matter what they tried or how hard they tried it, they still couldn't get the eleven-foot van to catch on the eleven-foot-nine door."

"Did they ever find out?" asked Kersey.

"Not as far as I know," said the wharf-and-rail bloke. "I got in just ahead of the boss and told him I was quitting on payday. Pat was going to have to take over my truck when I was gone, so they put him on as my offsider to fill the few days. And all day long he'd shake his head over the disgrace and shock of his first accident in over thirty years of driving. The last thing he said to me before I left was, 'The insurance company is going to pay out but I *still* don't know how it could possibly have happened.' And the last thing I said to him before I left was, 'Don't worry, Pat, I won't tell anyone. But I'd be careful what I said in front of the others, if I were you. I've got an idea they might just be inclined to be a little you-know-what with the boss.'

"Things are tough, all right," said Kersey.

"They're tough all right," agreed the wharf-and-rail bloke. "And they're going to get a lot worse before they get any better, by the looks of things."

They agreed another couple of times that things were tough all right, and a little while after that Kersey went to sleep. And when the foundry siren over at the railway workshops woke him up next morning, the wharf-and-rail bloke had already gone off to try and get another driving job.

That night, just as they were settling down, Kersey and the wharf-and-rail bloke thought they heard someone coming. They lay quiet and waited, listening.

And after a while a voice at the broken pane of the window said,

"I'm looking for my brother."

"Come round to the door and I'll let you in," said Kersey.

"I was wondering if my brother might be here," said the stranger, as he moved through the door past Kersey and stood in the darkness inside the gymnasium.

Kersey felt his way over to a pile of mats and slapped them to show the stranger where they were.

113

"Grab a couple of these and find yourself somewhere," he said. "Watch out you don't trip over anyone."

"Haven't you got a light in here?" said the new bloke, shuffling his way across the floor.

"We're not supposed to be in here," said Kersey. "We don't come here till after dark and we leave before daylight in the morning."

"Right," said the new bloke, dragging out two mats. "I heard there was a bunch of you blokes around here. Thought one of you might be my brother."

"What's he look like?" said the wharf-and-rail bloke.

"About the same size as me only four years younger, and a bit taller and heavier built."

"How the hell do we know what you look like?" said the wharf-and-rail bloke.

"No, he hasn't been here," said Kersey. "Where did you last see him?"

"Mangakino, just before the Christmas before last," said the new bloke. "He was coming over this way to paint a woolshed with a Maori bloke, but I've lost track of him altogether."

"He could be any bloody where," said the wharf-and-rail bloke, shrugging down into his mats.

"Yeah," agreed the new bloke. "I might run into him tomorrow," he added optimistically.

The new bloke came back the next night and set his mats up in his place on the floor as though he'd been booked in.

"Did you find out anything about your brother?" asked Kersey.

"No, not a thing," said the new bloke cheerfully.

"What does he do for a crust?" said the wharf-and-rail bloke.

"Same as me," said the new bloke, as though everyone knew.

"And what's that?" said Kersey curiously.

"Just about anything, same as our Old Man. He was a great worker, the Old Man. Nothing he wouldn't tackle. And he taught me brother and me the trade from the time we were old enough to walk. We worked from one end of the country to the other, mostly out in the backblocks because the Old Man didn't like cars and things much. He used to always say that the best way to do a thing was by hand, and he never turned a job down, no matter how tough it was."

"Where is he now?" asked Kersey.

"He retired about twelve years ago now," said the new bloke, thinking back. "My brother and I took over from him and he died of nothing to do about two years after that, and me mother and sister moved into the old shearers' quarters at Maungataniwha to live. Sister married a bloke. Shepherd over there."

"They might be able to put you on to that brother of yours," suggested the wharf-and-rail bloke.

"No, he wouldn't go there. Too much machinery. Everything's being done by machines over that way. That's what caused my brother and I to have to split up."

"Why?"

"Well, the Old Man didn't really know this, but by the time we took over from him things were starting to get tough in our line of business.

"When the Old Man died, me and me brother were splitting totara shingles and roofing sheds for cockies with them. But everyone was starting to reckon that the corrugated iron was cheaper and quicker, so we went on to splitting posts and battens. That lasted a while, until they started putting out all them sawn battens and treated pine posts and stuff and we couldn't compete with the prices. After that we took on a couple of fencing contracts, but we couldn't make enough out of it. Everyone else was using tractors and mechanical postholediggers; we couldn't handle stuff like that. The Old Man taught us how to do anything with a fishtail peg-and-drag and a team of horses, but by the time we grew up everything was being done with machines. We got born at a bad time, me brother reckons. A few years either way and we'd have been all right."

"But you can learn how to handle a tractor easy enough," pointed out the wharf-and-rail bloke.

"Yeah, but I don't like all this machinery and stuff anyway," said the new bloke. "Makes me nervous. You've only got to pick up a newspaper and see where someone's been killed or hurt by some tractor or something. And at the time there were still plenty of things we could do by hand, without getting involved with mechanical stuff. We did all right trapping rabbits for a while there. And when the rabbit boards took over we went on to possums. Made a good bit out of the skins, until they turned round and devalued them on us.

"It just seemed to happen to us. We'd tackle a thing and just when we'd be starting to make a real go of it, they'd invent something or turn out some new machine or other that'd make us superfluous again. Me brother and I had to split up in the finish. Not enough work in one place to keep us both going. He took on a contract to build a couple of swing bridges on a station down south, and after that I heard he wasn't going too bad on water-divining.

"I did a bit of droving on and off for about a year after that, but they gradually got the idea of shifting their stock around in them trucks. It's supposed to be quicker or something. I filled in a bit of time between droving jobs, packing supplies for mustering gangs and shoeing and breaking in horses and doing the odd bit of roadmakin' with the horse-scoop — things like that.

"But in the finish I had to sell me dogs. There just weren't enough drovin' jobs to be worth keepin' them. But I had a pretty good spin on sowin' grass-seed and superphosphate by hand on some of that steep country around Hawke's Bay. Just used to open up the bags and sow the stuff straight off the packhorses. As a matter of fact I was the only one doin' that kind of work on contract around there. And there was a fair bit of other work goin' to keep me busy between contracts. When they were cuttin' their hay I was in big demand because I could build a better haystack than any of them. It's a dyin' art these days, haystack buildin'.

"And then they brought out them red machines and everyone started getting their hay done up in bales. And on top of that they went and brought in this aerial top dressin' with them aeroplanes. I reckon they'd be better off puttin' the stuff on by hand, but they still go zoomin' all over the countryside in their aeroplanes, scattering the stock and crashin' into things. It's supposed to be quicker than doin' it by hand but they must lose a fair bit of time cartin' out their dead aeroplane-drivers and cleanin' up after all the crashes they have. It doesn't make a hell of a lot of difference to me if they want to risk their lives for a couple of bags of super.

"I got a good price for me packhorses and took on a bit of

rush-cuttin' and ragwort-pullin'. Things like that. It wasn't bad for a while, but then they got to inventin' all them chemicals and things to spray the stuff with. And them drain-diggin' machines they've got now cut into our work a lot. There used to be a lot of money to be made keepin' drains open.

"There's still a bit of saw-doctorin' and horse-shoein' and the odd stockwhip or saddle to make. And you can get a job swingin' the old banjo on the road works sometimes, but you have to watch it on that job, believe me. The way they drive them cars these days — especially them red ones! It's bloody dangerous. Just as well the Old Man's not around to see what's happenin', I can tell you.

"And things are gettin' worse. In some places they're even usin' motorbikes instead of horses for musterin' and riding the lambin'-beat. They don't even cut a boxthorn hedge by hand now, it's all being done with machines. I used to be not too bad on fixing windmills and water-pumps but it's that long since I've seen one I don't know if I could remember. Everyone's going in for these electricity jobs these days. And different types and makes of the same sort of machines being handed out all the time . . . I wonder how me brother's gettin' on," said the new bloke, pausing thoughtfully.

"Have you ever thought of having a go at something different?" said Kersey helpfully.

"Nar, wouldn't dream of it," said the new bloke. "It's not half as bad as it sounds. There's still quite a few things bein' done by hand. And there will be for a good while yet. Don't take any notice of me. As a matter of fact, I've had a bit of bad luck just lately."

"You don't say," said the wharf-and-rail bloke.

"Yes," said the do-it-by-hand bloke seriously. "I just lost a damn good job through sheer rotten luck."

"What was it?"

"Shootin' deer and packin' out the venison. Down on the West Coast. Twelve cents a pound at the road, we were gettin' for it."

"Don't tell me they've mechanised that," said the wharf-and-rail bloke.

"No, no," said the do-it-by-hand bloke. "There wasn't a machine for miles. No, it was far worse than that. It was blowflies."

"Did you say *blowflies*?" said the wharf-and-rail bloke.

"Too right I did," said the do-it-by-hand bloke, flouncing vigorously in his bed of mats. "They done for me good and proper. I tell you, you blokes reckon you've had it tough, but you don't know what tough is till you've run up against them West Coast blowflies. There's hordes of 'em, they come from everywhere. They had me rooted from the start — and they knew it," he added indignantly. "A man's got no show once he runs up against them there West Coast blowflies," he concluded philosophically.

"Much in this meat-hunting caper?" asked Kersey.

"There would've been if it wasn't for them blowflies," said the new bloke. "They're fair dinkum murder down there, I tell you."

"Blow all your meat or something, did they?"

"You're not kiddin' they blew all me meat. It wasn't so bad when I was gettin' a few deer down near the road. But they got a bit too scarce and scary in all the handy country, so I started huntin' from a hut two and a half hours up the valley.

"The first night up there I shot four deer out on the river flats,

119

just on dark, and I carted the carcases back to the hut on a couple of horses I'd borrowed off a cocky down at the road. Hung the meat in a tree there. Next morning I got another three deer and by the time I got 'em back to the hut the four I'd got the night before were goners."

"Blowflies?" said the wharf-and-rail bloke.

"Blowflies! You never seen the likes of it. Couldn't believe me eyes at first. I tell you, it looked like four enormous swarms of bees hangin' in the tree there. You could hardly see the carcases — white with blowfly eggs they were. No hope of savin' 'em. I cut 'em down and dragged 'em across and slung 'em in the river. Could hardly see for the clouds of blowflies. About twelve or fourteen dollars' worth of meat down the drain, not countin' all my hard work.

"Fair go, it'd break your heart. And by the time I got back to the hut they'd got stuck into the three carcases I still had on the horses. Dirty great clouds of 'em, roarin' around the horses. I belted into 'em with a sack but I had to give it in because it was makin' the horses jumpy."

"What did you do?" asked Kersey.

"I covered the loads as best as I could, with sacks and bits of tentage and my good sleepin'-bag cover, and took off down the river to get the meat into a big safe we had down at the road while there was still time."

"Did you make it?" asked the wharf-and-rail bloke.

"Did I make it? — Like hell I did! Never had a dog's show against them bloody blowflies. I tell you, they're diabolical, that's what they are — diabolical. By the time I'd got an hour and a half down the river I knew I wasn't goin' to make it. They blew the meat and they blew the sacks and the tentage and me good sleepin'-bag cover. They blew the horses and the pack-saddles — the whole outfit was covered with great clusters of blowfly eggs. My three carcases were done for. I cut 'em down off the horses and dragged 'em across and slung 'em in the river."

"I didn't know they'd blow leather and things like that," said Kersey.

"They'll blow *anything*, mate, them West Coast blowflies," said the new bloke. "By the time I got back to the hut and hobbled the horses they'd blown the spuds and the onions and even got stuck into me spare pair of socks I had hangin' in front of the fireplace.

"Things being what they are as far as getting jobs goes, I couldn't afford to let them blowflies beat me. There were plenty of deer around up there. I was on to a good thing once I had the flies licked. First off I tried hangin' the meat in the smoke — kept a fire going under it all night and half the next day, but the blowflies seemed to prefer it that way. In the finish I had to cut it down and drag it across and sling it in the river.

"Then I decided to try a lurk someone had put me on to once. Everyone knows that blowflies can't go any higher than about fifteen feet above the ground. The next night I took the horses up the river and got five deer in no time. Packed the carcases back to the hut, swipin' at the blowflies all the way, and slung ropes through the forks of trees and hoisted all the meat right up — about twenty or thirty feet. It was dark by the time I'd done this but I couldn't see any blowflies around up there."

"Did that work?" asked the wharf-and-rail bloke.

"Did it work? — Like hell it did," said the new bloke. "I tell you, if you air-dropped a leg of meat from two thousand feet among them West Coast blowflies, it'd land with maggots on it. By the time I got up next morning it was too late. It's a wonder how the ropes stood up to the extra weight!"

"Hell, what did you do?" asked Kersey.

"I cut 'em down and dragged 'em across and slung 'em in the river," said the new bloke. "All except one carcase that was hangin' in the tree beside the hut. The rope had pulled into the fork of the tree so tight it wouldn't run out when I tried to let it down. Jammed there, it was. And there was no show of me gettin' up there to free it. The tree was too big to think of cuttin' it down. I tried to shoot the rope out of the fork but I had to turn it in. Couldn't spare the ammunition. So the bloody thing had to stay there."

"Spare me days," said the wharf-and-rail bloke. "I bet that lot stunk after a while?"

"Stunk!" said the new bloke. "You're not kidding it stunk. It probably kept some of them blowflies away from me tucker, though. A man's got to be wide awake to get a feed past them West Coast blowflies, y'know. They'll dive-bomb a forkful of bully-beef half a dozen times between the tin and your mouth."

"Hell," said Kersey. "No wonder you had to chuck it in."

"Oh, I didn't chuck it in then," said the new bloke. "I wasn't goin' to let a few million blowflies do me out of me livin'. And besides, I still had a trick or two up me sleeve."

"But how were you going to get your meat down to the road, even if you could keep the flies off it?" said the wharf-and-rail bloke.

"Yeah," said Kersey. "Wouldn't they get at it on the way, like they did the first time?"

"Ah — that's just it," said the new bloke. "Everyone knows

that blowflies can't operate in the dark. I could pack the stuff out at night, and no trouble. The horses knew the track and it was easy goin' most of the way. All I had to do was keep them off it during the daytime. So I dug a hole."

"A hole?"

"Yeah, a real big one. Took me two days to get it right. Then I laid four fresh carcases in it on rails and put boards across the top and covered the whole thing with sacks and dirt. It was absolutely pitch black in there — I looked."

"That was a crafty move," said Kersey.

"Not crafty enough for them West Coast blowflies," said the new bloke grimly.

"Don't tell us they got in there too," said the wharf and-rail bloke incredulously.

"They not only got in there, mate, they waited till I was out of the way before they did it. I watched that hole for a good twenty minutes after I put the meat in it, just to make dead sure, and there were no more blowflies around it than any other area the same size around there. And when I got back that evening with another couple of carcases to make up a full load to smuggle out to the road that night, I could hear 'em roarin' away in that hole twenty yards away."

"Was the meat ruined?" asked Kersey.

"Never even bothered to look, mate. I just filled the hole in on top of it."

"Is that when you quit?" asked the wharf-and-rail bloke.

"No," replied the new bloke. "Me professional pride wouldn't let me give in to 'em. I had enough tucker left to last another couple of days, and if I could get just one load of venison down to the road I'd make enough out of it to stock up again and buy gauze and stuff to build a proper flyproof meat-safe up the river. So I played me last card.

"I shot six deer along the river and as soon as I got the carcases cleaned up I dragged 'em across and slung 'em in the river and weighed 'em down with rocks and marked the places where they were. You should have seen them blowflies! Angry as hell, they were. Buzzin' and swoopin' and circlin' around over where the meat was. I reckon some of 'em even had a go at blowin' the river when I wasn't looking. But I had 'em bluffed this time.

"Just to make dead certain, I waited till about an hour after dark that night before I sneaked out and saddled up the horses. There were still a few blowflies bombardin' around in the hut when I left, but that was only because of the light from a candle I'd had goin' in there. Outside there wasn't a blowfly to be seen or heard anywhere — except the odd bunch that roared off like mobs of quail when I picked up a sack or a packsaddle or anything that'd been lying around.

"I got the meat loaded up and took off for the road without seeing or hearing a single blowfly, hardly. Got there about midnight and hung the meat in the safe and camped there.

"And next morning when I went to trim up the venison for the factory bloke it just about broke me heart."

"Blowflies?" asked Kersey and the wharf-and-rail bloke almost at once.

"No, mate. Maggots, Thousands of 'em. Bloody whoppers, right through the lot. Everywhere they were — droppin' off on to the ground."

"What did you do?" asked Kersey.

"What did I do? I cut 'em down and dragged 'em across and

slung 'em in the river, that's what I did. Then I took the horses back to the bloke I'd borrowed 'em off and got a lift to town with the venison bloke when he came. Professional pride or not, a man's got to know when he's cut his load. You've got to hand it to them West Coast blowflies, though. They're fair dinkum diabolical, that's what they are. Bloody diabolical!"

"So that's how you came to be here," said Kersey.

"Yeah mate. That's right. I registered for the dole down south but I couldn't stay on there. Had to get out of it."

"How come?" asked Kersey curiously.

"Well, it was like this, mate," said the new bloke. "I was a bit light for a feed so I decided to try the old maggot trick on a restaurant. And you've got no idea the trouble I had trying to get hold of an ordinary maggot. There's no justice. I finally rounded up a weedy lookin' specimen and put it in a matchbox and went into that flash new place on Curnew Street there. Had a slap-up feed of steak, eggs, onions, chips, tomatoes and three lots of bread and butter. And when I'd finished I put me maggot on the side of the plate and yelled out for the waitress."

"What did she do?" asked the wharf-and-rail bloke.

"She went and got the cook, but he wouldn't wear it. Great big joker he was, too. Reckoned that if the maggot had been in the tucker it wouldn't be still alive. I could see that he had his mind made up about it so I didn't bother stayin' around to argue with him. They followed me for a while but I lost 'em down around the waterfront .

"I kept out of the way till I got me dole money and then I caught the train to here — and here I am," concluded the blowfly bloke.

THIRTEEN

Flower Arrangement

I was travelling south to meet Dan with the car. The first to arrive at the Fentonbridge Hotel was to book us both in and then wait for the other. It looked as though Dan would be there well before me, as I'd been held up and wouldn't arrive at the hotel until late that night.

I was bowling along at a fair speed, trying to make up a bit of time, when I saw the hitch-hiker on the road ahead, thumbing for a lift. I wouldn't have bothered wasting time with hitch-hikers, except that this one was a girl, a young one, and on her own. Good-looking too, and not *too* young. So I stopped and picked her up.

She was passing through the town I was going to and by the time we arrived there, at about half past ten that night, we were getting quite friendly. We'd been to different schools together. She was on a kind of working holiday and was looking for work as she'd almost run out of money.

I drove straight to the hotel and put the car in the parking lot at the back.

"My mate will have booked me in here," I told her. "Why don't you do a ringbolt in my room? It's a hell of a night to spend out and there's no point in paying for hotel accommodation when you can get in for nothing. You can sneak out early in the morning and no one'll be any the wiser."

She had a few half-hearted objections at first. She had a sleeping-bag . . . She didn't usually . . . She might get caught. The usual guff. She didn't take much persuading. It had been raining up until an hour or so before and it was a freezing cold night.

I left her to wait in the car and went round to the lobby of the hotel and rang a buzzer at the receptionist's counter. A fussy, thin, pimply, dapper little chap came through a door into the office.

"Yes sir?" he lisped.

"Name's Watson," I told him. "Has Mr Curtis booked me in here?"

"Yes, I think so, sir. I'll just check."

He opened the usual big book on the counter. "Let's see now — yes, here it is. You and Mr Curtis are in woom seventeen. It's the fourth on the left at the top of the stairs."

This was a bit awkward.

"Ah — you haven't put us both in the same room, have you?" I asked.

"Oh yes, sir. I remember Mr Curtis especially asked for a double woom."

In spite of him spraying a fair bit of spit around as he talked, I leaned over towards him and said, "Look, I don't want to cast any aspersions on Mr Curtis's character, he's a very nice man, but — well, it's just that I'd rather have a room of my own, that's all. You see . . ." I whispered confidentially in his twitching ear for a few moments.

His response was, I thought, a bit on the drastic side.

"Well," he said, after a short pause for what appeared to be intense concentration. "That is exactly what I suspected. I knew there was something wong with that man the very moment he walked into this hotel. Disgwaceful, absolutely disgwaceful! Don't you wowwy, Mr Watson, I'll find a sepawate woom for you. Disgusting. That's what it is. Disgusting. If the manager

128

was to discover what kind of — person — was under his woof, I don't know what he'd think."

"I don't think it'd be a very good idea to tell anyone about it," I said quickly. "Let's just keep it to ourselves, eh?"

The receptionist drew himself up to his full five foot six or seven, aimed his Adam's apple right between my eyes and said, "I have no desire to discuss such things with anyone, sir." And after a short pause for effect he began to look through his big book for a room to put me in.

I was eventually installed in "woom nineteen", right next to the one Dan was in. The little receptionist, with several more "disgustings", a "disgwaceful" or two, and an "outwageous", left me with a conspiratorial warning not to make any noise and "awouse that man in the next woom".

I had the uncomfortable feeling that my little white lie was being taken entirely too seriously, but I didn't worry too much about it just then. I had other things on my mind.

I gave the receptionist about half an hour to get clear of the lobby and then went out and smuggled my freezing hitch-hiker up the stairs and into the room — and out again at about half past five next morning. It wasn't worth all the trouble I'd gone to. She made me wait in the shower while she got into bed, and then generously gave me a blanket and pointed out how comfortable the chair looked. When I tried to point out to her the various advantages of double beds, she threatened to scream if I so much as laid a finger on her. I couldn't risk calling her bluff. I'd stuck my neck out far enough as it was.

I got in about an hour's sleep after she left and heard Dan moving around in his room while I was still straightening things up in mine. I rang him up on the telephone.

"Hullo," I heard him say through the wall.

"Hullo, Dan," I said. "Dick here. Where are you?"

"Room seventeen," he replied. "What the hell happened to you yesterday? Where are you?"

"Got in late," I said. "They put me in room nineteen. — Hey, that must be somewhere near where you are."

"Next door," said Dan. "Aren't they beauts! I told them to put you in here with me."

"They must have a different receptionist on at night," I said. "He probably didn't know about it."

"The bloke who jacked it up wouldn't know whether he was Arthur or Martha," said Dan. "Did you get everything fixed up before you left Ingleton?"

"Yep."

"Right, I'll see you at breakfast. We'll get away from here as soon as we can. We've lost enough time on this trip as it is. Can't afford any more holdups."

"Okay."

It looked as though I was going to get away with it.

In the diningroom Dan was sitting alone at a table. The waitress sat me with him as though she was directing me to a brothel. We talked about the stupid inefficiency of the hotel until our breakfast was brought and flung down on the table as though the waitress was dealing us a hand of poker. While we were eating lambs' fry and bacon Dan suddenly stopped and looked around the other occupied tables.

"What the hell's everyone staring at us for?" he hissed.

"Staring at us?" I said, as surprised as I could manage. "You must be imagining things. I haven't noticed anyone staring at us," I lied.

Dan looked around again and then went on eating. Then a few minutes later he dropped his knife and fork on the table.

"What the hell is wrong with everyone around here?" he snarled. "They *are* staring at us."

"Garn," I said uncomfortably. "You must be a bit on edge this morning."

"There's something queer about this dump," he announced. "I'm not staying here again, that's for sure."

Then the manager of the hotel appeared at our table and addressed himself to Dan.

"We don't encourage your type in the hotel, Mr Curtis," he said stiffly. "I would like you to vacate your room as soon as possible — and I wouldn't bother trying to seek accommodation here again, if I were you."

And he turned and walked out of the room, leaving Dan sitting there stunned and speechless. And me squirming in my chair.

"What the hell's crawling on him?" Dan finally managed to gasp.

"Damned if I know," I said. "Let's get out of here. They're all crazy. It's no good trying to reason with nuts like that."

"Nuts is right," said Dan with a bewildered glance around the silent diningroom. "The whole place is crazy. I've a good mind to demand an explanation."

I only just managed to convince him it would be a waste of time. We left the diningroom and collected our odds and ends from our rooms. The dapper little receptionist bloke came in answer to the buzzer, looking as though he'd just discovered a nasty smell.

"Yes, sir?" he sniffed.

"Want to pay our bill," I said shortly. I'd like to have had a chat with him about keeping his big mouth shut, but with Dan standing there in the explosive state he was in it was out of the question. The best thing to do was get out of there as quickly as possible.

"Seven dollars, eighty-five," intoned the receptionist, slapping the receipt book on the counter as though it was someone's face.

I paid him and took the receipt. We were just turning away towards the front door when he suddenly held up a pair of black, lacy panties, delicately pinched between finger and thumb.

"These were found in your bedclothes by the house maid," he said to me. "We don't want such things here."

Dan croaked some astonished thing and I grabbed the panties the receptionist was waving in my face and stuffed them in my pocket out of sight.

I shouldn't have admitted knowing anything about those pants, but they'd taken me by surprise. It was too late now. Dan followed me out of the hotel with a look of grim curiosity that was going to demand satisfying.

I was desperately trying to think of a way to square off with Dan when we came in sight of the car. My hitch-hiker was sprawled out on the front seat with her feet on the window. Waiting for a lift, she said.

Dan took one look and really did his block. He didn't even bother to ask what had really been going on, or give me a chance to explain. No one would have believed me anyway, come to think of it.

That's why I'm back in here. You see, I was only allowed out on probation as long as Dan guaranteed my good behaviour.

It just doesn't seem fair somehow.

FOURTEEN
A Stroke of Luck

Windy Long had had a stroke of luck and wound up at a party in Ngongotaha.

There was a bloke, mill-worker by the look of him, who'd latched on to them. Everyone thought he was with one of the others. Windy didn't go much on the look of him in the first place, but it wasn't him who'd invited him to the party. Nor had anyone else, as far as they could work out later. He just tagged along and when things were starting to get warmed up, around one o'clock in the morning, this bloke whose name nobody knew decided to get crook. He was sitting in a big old armchair that everybody reckoned later should have been given to one of the women, only no one thought to say anything about it at the time.

He started getting a bit wild in the eye at first. Then he looked around worried and swallowing and shifting his bottle of beer round on the carpet from one side of his chair to the other. Then he got to gurgling and waving and trying to get out of the chair.

Puketu and the boys would have just shunted him outside for a look around and a bit of fresh air and left him to it, but not Mrs Puketu. She fussed around him like an old mother hen, telling him what was wrong with him and what to do about it.

"A nice big feed. That's what you need," she said, helping him on to his feet. "I'll just bet you haven't had a decent meal all day. Now you take this plate and go out to the stove and help yourself to some lovely hot stew. There's a whole big pot of it. Nice mutton stew, with carrots and parsnips and kumara and puha."

The bloke took the plate and spoon as though he was hypnotised and wandered into the kitchen. He lifted the lid of the pot on the woodstove and as soon as the steam from the stew hit him in the face he cut loose. All over the hot stove. Then he sat down against the wall by the stove and passed out, dribbling all over his shirt as though it happened every day. Everybody crowded into the kitchen doorway, looking at this character and the terrible mess he'd made. Then it started to pong.

It pongs a bit when you burn rubber or hair. It pongs when you're stripping the wool of a dead sheep, or the knife slips when you're gutting a poisoned cow. Cattle trucks pong and so do rotten cabbages. Everybody's got their pet pong that they can't stand, but this was the pongingest pong Windy had ever tried not to smell. It was so bad that he was scared to take his next breath, and then it didn't matter because he couldn't. It went through the house like rotten steam under pressure. Everybody reeled back into the sitting-room. Puketu threw a couple of buckets of water at the stove but it was as much use as trying to put out a fire with diesel oil.

The party was a goner. It occurred to Windy at the time that it'd be a hell of a good way to bust up a party that wasn't going too well, but a bit on the drastic side. It would have stopped a riot.

They took the beer outside and stood around Windy's van, drinking and arguing who ought to go in and drag out the bloke who done it before he got asphyxiated and pegged out all over Mrs Puketu's kitchen floor. That was when they found out he'd never been invited in the first place.

In the finish, Windy ducked in and dragged him out to the

porch and threw a coat over him and left him there to sleep it off. Then he shifted the van a little further away from the house and they carried on with the party, which was beginning to pick up a little. Puketu lit a big fire and business was almost back to normal.

Around daylight they were down to the last few bottles and everyone was getting sleepy. Mrs Puketu took Puketu by the ear and led him gently up to the house to do a bit of mop-swinging and the rest of them decided to blow. Puketu called out that their guest of honour had gone from the porch. He must have woken up and slunk off somewhere.

Windy drove some of the other blokes in to Rotorua, gassed up his van and took off for Auckland, where he'd decided to look for work. At the bottom of a long hill he saw a bloke on the side of the road, thumbing a lift. He was nearly past before he recognised him. It was the feed-of-stew bloke, padding the hoof for Tokoroa or Putaruru, most likely. Poor sod must have been stony. Windy pulled up to give him a lift. They'd been a bit rough on him the night before. He was probably only lonely and wanted a bit of company. Can't blame a bloke for that, really, Windy thought to himself, it could even have happened to me.

As his hitch-hiker came up to the van Windy reached over to open the door for him.

"Hop in. Where are you going?"

The bloke got in, slammed the door as hard as he could, and snarled: "It's about time one of you bastards stopped. You've been going past for bloody hours."

This knocked Windy back a bit. The only time this bloke had opened his mouth the night before it was to spew on Mrs

Puketu's stove, and now he was packing a snotty. "It's not me who's been going past for hours, mate."

"Ar, you're all the bloody same," said the bloke. And he opened the door and slammed it again.

"Where are you going?" Windy asked him again.

"You got any cigarettes in this thing?" said the bloke, opening the glovebox and poking around among Windy's things in there.

Windy would never see a man stuck for a smoke.

"Yes, there's some rolls on the seat here. Help yourself."

"Haven't you got any tailormades?"

"No."

The bloke opened the door again and slammed it as hard as he could again. "Don't go so fast," he said. "You'll make a man nervous."

"That door's okay," Windy said shortly. "You don't have to slam it all the time."

"Don't trust the bloody things."

"Where do you want to get off?" Windy asked impatiently.

"Did you bring any beer?" the bloke asked, ignoring Windy's question.

"There's a bottle or two in the carton in the back here," said Windy, a bit put off. "You should be able to reach it over the back of the seat."

"Where are you going?" asked the bloke, not reaching for the beer.

"Auckland," said Windy. "What about you?"

"What part? Auckland's a bloody big place."

"Takapuna," said Windy at random.

"Got your own place?"

"No. I stay with friends there."

"That'll do," said the bloke, settling into the seat.

"Now look here, mate," said Windy. "You're not staying with me and that's flat. There's not enough room for you and I'm only a guest there myself. Just tell where you want to go and I'll drop you off there."

Again the bloke opened the door and slammed it.

"And you can stop slamming that damn door," Windy said hotly. "You'll end up breaking it. Now where do you want to be let off?"

"Do you believe in God?" asked the bloke.

When Windy recovered from his surprise he said: "I never discuss my religious views in public."

The man was obviously as mad as a meat-axe.

"I thought as much. All you religious blokes are the same. Talk big about helping your fellow men, but you'd charge a dying man for a drink of water if you owned a river."

"Now look here, mate . . ." began Windy.

"You needn't bother preaching your sermons to me," said the bloke, waving his hand in Windy's ear. "I've been listening to you blokes for years and I've never run into one of you yet who practised what he preached. A pack of hypocrites, that's what you are. A pack of bloody hypocrites!"

This was getting too much altogether. "If there's any more of that kind of talk you can get out and walk," said Windy.

"Seventh Day Adventists," announced the bloke. "I can pick 'em a mile off."

The bloke was off his rocker all right. Windy decided to kid him along till they got to Hamilton and put him off there. He was a fairly hefty bloke and Windy didn't want any trouble with him.

"You're wrong," he said for a joke. "Salvation Army."

"In that case you won't mind lending me five dollars when we get to Auckland," he said.

"Like hell," said Windy angrily. "You're not getting any five dollars off me. I'll give you a lift as far as Hamilton."

The bloke didn't seem to be able to hear what he didn't want to. He slammed the door again and picked up Windy's tobacco and started rolling thin smokes, which he carefully put in his shirt pocket.

"You might as well keep the packet," Windy told him after a while.

"Don't need your charity," said the bloke, shaking the last of the tobacco into the corner of the packet for one more smoke out of it. He put that one in his mouth and lit it, pocketing Windy's matches when he'd used them for the job. Then he threw the empty tobacco packet out the window and reached into the back of the van for a bottle of beer.

"Where's your opener?" he demanded, dragging a bottle out of the carton.

"On the key-ring," said Windy. "Here y'are." He passed him the opener.

"Any glasses?" he wanted to know.

"What do you think?" Windy asked him sarcastically. "Do I look the kind of bloke who carts glasses around with him? You can drink out of the bottle, same as I do."

He did drink out of the bottle. Every drop of it. And when Windy asked him politely if it would be too much trouble to offer him a drink, he said: "Not on your life. Your driving's bad enough as it is, without boozing on top of it."

"You don't have to put up with it," Windy pointed out. "You

can get out and walk any time you like."

"Shut your window," said the bloke. "It's as cold as hell in here. You want a man to catch pneumonia or something and wind up in hospital?"

They arrived at a small town and Windy's passenger said: "I'm hungry. How about you?"

It was the first time he'd taken Windy into consideration and Windy felt ridiculously touched by it.

"Yeah, starving," he said.

"Well, pull up here and I'll get something to eat," said the bloke magnificently.

Windy stopped by a little shop that said they sold pies and things and the bloke got out and went into the shop. He came back eating a pie, with another one in a paper bag. He got in, slammed the door as hard as he could and said: "Right. Let's get going."

Once they were under way again Windy reached out for the other pie, but the bloke grabbed it off the seat and put it in his lap.

"No, you don't," he said indignantly. "If you wanted a pie you should have got one when we were at that shop back there."

Windy pulled over to the side of the road and stopped.

"Righto, mate," he said. "This is as far as you go. Out you get."

The bloke opened the door and Windy thought for a moment that he was going to leave without any trouble, but he only wanted to slam it again.

"You might wait till I finish me pie," he said, throwing the crust from the first pie on the floor and starting on the second.

They sat there in silence while he slowly ate the pie. When

he'd finished dropping crust on the seat and floor, Windy got out and went round to his side and opened the door.

"Come on, mate. Out!" He was determined that this bloke wasn't going to talk him out of it this time.

The man got a smoke out of his shirt pocket and carefully lit it. When it was going properly he stepped out on to the roadside and looked at the sky.

"I hope the next driver is a bit more sociable than you," he said. And he walked off in the direction they'd just come from without looking back or another word. Windy got back into the van and drove quickly away without looking back.

A few miles later he saw another man walking and didn't take much notice of him, but when he got close he saw that he was well-dressed, and he turned and smiled for a lift. Windy had been getting a bit sleepy, and a bit of a yarn was just what he needed to keep him awake. So he stopped.

The man put his bag on the floor and got in, closing the door so carefully it wouldn't latch properly and Windy had to tell him to slam it.

"Where are you heading for?" he asked.

"The next settlement will do, thank you," said the man.

He was a quiet sort of bloke this one. He didn't say another word for about a mile and Windy was working out how to get a conversation going when the man suddenly said:

"Do you believe in God, sir?"

Windy nearly went off the road.

"Er — why?" he managed to say.

"Well you see, I'm going around making sure that there is a Bible in every home I visit, so that people are always in touch with the Lord. If you haven't a Bible I'll be happy to provide you with one. We don't charge anything but if people feel that they'd like to make a small contribution towards our work we are always happy to accept it. You see, we feel that if everybody has access to God, whether they make use of it or not, it will be a great step towards better understanding. You'd be surprised at the number of people who turn to the Lord in times of trouble and hardship and loneliness. People who never go to church from one year to the next. For them the Bible represents . . ."

And he went on and on and onandonandon . . . Windy was having trouble keeping his eyes on the road, and the sound of the man's voice was only making him sleepier. He thought of stopping for a spell, and he most likely would have if he hadn't had the passenger. He decided to wait till he got him where he was going and then pull into a side road for a spell.

He didn't make it. Windy didn't know exactly what happened. One minute he was driving along and the next he was lying in some grass with glass everywhere and people standing around talking urgently.

Two policemen came to see him in hospital and get a statement. Windy couldn't tell them as much as they told him. He'd run off the road on a corner. Going too fast to take it, they said. The van was a write-off.

"Were you insured, sir?"

"No."

"That's unfortunate."

Windy's passenger was in the same hospital, pretty badly knocked around, they said. His door had sprung open and he'd been thrown out.

The police said they'd found an empty beer bottle in the van and some broken full ones. Windy had smelled strongly of liquor when he was dragged from the wreck, and on this evidence there was some talk of bringing charges of drunken driving, or at least negligent driving against him.

"You're lucky not to be being charged with something even more serious than that, sir. Manslaughter."

Somehow Windy couldn't help blaming the bloke who was sick on Mrs Puketu's stove. If it hadn't been for him Windy would at least have had a feed before he set off. Then he'd smoked all Windy's smokes and drunk all the beer and ate all the pies and kept slamming the van door. If it hadn't been for him he might even have had a bit of sleep at Puketu's place the night before. But how could he ever explain a thing like that to the police? He couldn't even *tell* them about him: he'd make a great witness!

No. It was just a typical run of Windy's luck. He'd lost his van and he lost his driver's licence for three years.

So much for his stroke of luck. If Aunt Meredith hadn't left him all that money, he wouldn't have bought the van and ended up at Puketu's place and run into the door-slamming bloke and ended up on the way to Auckland, where he met up with the religious bloke who talked him to sleep and caused him to run off the road.

No, the stroke of luck wasn't Windy being left all that money. The stroke of luck was when the magistrate lost patience with trying to get some sense out of him and dismissed him on the negligent driving charge the police had brought against him.

FIFTEEN

OVERHEARD IN THE PUB

"Thanks, mate. Y'know, I don't mind accepting your shout. It could easy be me who's shouting you. . . . Yep, if it hadn't been for a shower of rain I'd be one of the wealthiest men in the Territory today.

"A shower of rain was unusual enough, out there beyond Alice Springs, but what that rain done to me shouldn't have happened to a dog. Cost me a fortune, just like that, it did. — Y'see, it was like this. Last year I decided to take a couple of weeks off and treat meself to a little holiday away from all the dust and heat and flies. So I sets off for the coast, Surfer's Paradise, to have meself a good time. — Yeah, thanks, I will have another beer. Ta.

"Well, after a couple of days I got a bit jack of all the noise and racket goin' on round the place, so I took meself for a walk along the beach away from all the crowds. And I was just wanderin' along thinkin' about goin' home when a dirty big wave came and washed a fish up on the beach right at me feet. Sand mullet, it was — about this long. Now here's a go, I says to meself. And I picks up this here sand mullet and carts it back to the pub I was stayin' in to show everyone how I'd caught a fish without even a fishin' line. No one seemed to be very impressed about it.

"The fish was still kinda floppin' around a bit so for somethin' to do I got a four-gallon kerosene tin and filled it with sea water and put me sand mullet in. It started floppin' around

145

in there and pretty soon it was swimmin' about as though it had never been out of the water. After a couple of days I had the thing eating out of me hand. And some of the stuff that thing ate, you just wouldn't believe. Leaves and grass, steak, mutton chops, bread and jam, scrambled eggs, porridge, cigarette butts, chocolate — anything you liked to throw in, that sand mullet of mine'd up and eat it without turnin' a hair.

"Then I got the idea of takin' me fish back to the station, out beyond the Alice there, to show the folks. Some of 'em had never seen the sea in their lives, let alone a real live fish. So I hops on the train with me swag and me kerosene tin with me sand mullet in it.

"Feedin' the thing was no trouble, I just bought it a couple of sandwiches or a pie or somethin' when we stopped for refreshments. But as we got further out into the hot country the water in me kerosene tin started evaporatin'. I didn't have any spare sea water with me so I just had to top her up with fresh water. The sand mullet didn't seem to take any notice of this, and by the time we got out to Alice Springs he was swimmin' around in fresh water as though he'd been born to it.

"When I got me fish out to the station there was a hell of a stir-up. Everyone wanted to pick it up and see what it felt like. I tried to warn them it was supposed to stay under the water or it'd die but they wouldn't take any notice. After a bit me poor old sand mullet got pretty used to bein' picked up and passed around to be looked at, because people from all over were comin' to have a look.

"Then there was a dirty big drought and we couldn't spare the water to keep fillin' up the sand mullet's kerosene tin. So we made it half full, and then a quarter full — and in the end he got

so used to it that I just used to throw a wet sack over him and he laid there good as gold. In the finish he was floppin' around the yard with fowls, pickin' up all the scraps and fowl tucker he could get his hands on. The old rooster got pretty jealous of him in the finish and they had a ding-dong donnybrook out in the yard one day. The sand mullet was doin' pretty good for himself, too. I had to stop the fight in case he knocked off our only breedin' rooster.

"Well, word got around about me sand mullet and a bloke from Melbourne flew up in his private plane and took one look and made me an offer of five thousand dollars for it, but I could see by this time I was sittin' on a goldmine, so I turned 'im down flat. Then I started gettin' phone calls from big outfits all over the world — Thanks, yes, a big one, barman — wantin' me sand mullet. I accepted an offer of thirty thousand dollars from a film company in America in the finish. I was supposed to fly over to deliver me sand mullet and collect the dough. The night before I was due to set off, the drought broke. The heaviest rain in the Territory for thirty years. I was quite pleased in a way because I could put me fish back into his kero tin to transport him, now we had the water. So I got everything ready and arranged for a plane to pick us up in the morning and fly us over to Brisbane, where we could take off for the States.

"And you know, mate — you mightn't believe this, but it's as true as I'm standing here — when I went out in the morning to get me poor old sand mullet, he'd fallen into a puddle of water and drowned himself."

SIXTEEN

Hot Stuff

About eighteen feet by twelve; four-by-two frame and corrugated iron. An axe stuck in a worn-away woodblock surrounded by chips and bits of firewood — the nearest thing to a garden it was ever likely to have.

To a city woman the old roadman's hut would have been nothing less than unsightly chaos, but from Squinty Bill's angle it was a good camp, and he was the one who had to live in it. Had lived in it for years. Everything had its place and uses. Even the big stone on the floor by the wall was to hold the door open on hot days, or when he needed more light inside. The sacks on the steps, the porch, the floor and the window all served an obviously useful purpose, and the ones hanging on the fence outside were spares.

The pile of passed-on magazines and newspapers in the cardboard box at the foot of the bed was for lighting fires, and the bed itself sagged in the middle where it was always sat on, just enough so your feet comfortably reached the floor. Nails for hanging things on were banged into the unlined timbers with things hanging on them. A bow-saw, spare hats and old elbowy jackets; a big frying-pan; a rabbit trap; a coil of fuse; a two-year old Dalgety's calendar, with a picture of a place where Squinty Bill had worked once; a mended bridle; a semi-retired rifle rusted patiently in a corner alongside a curly stick waiting to be carved into a walking stick for his old age. Things like that.

His good clothes hung on a single hanger in the space

149

between a corner and a tall cupboard, with his going-to-town shoes on the floor beneath. The table was under the window with a row of sauce bottles and salt and pepper tins against the wall at the back. An up-ended box and two chairs with sack seats made one part-time and two permanent seats. Oilskins, gumboots, shovels, slasher and pick on the porch, and the bachelor smells of damp clothing, tobacco, woodsmoke and meths and kero for the Tilley lamp gave the place a dim, wet-weather atmosphere.

Squinty Bill himself was one of those men who seemed to have been in the bush longer than the trees. He had, so to speak, cut his teeth on a whetstone. There were no teeth left now but he was a tough old rag, for all his age. And what he didn't know about huts and camps hadn't cropped up in the last sixty years or so.

Admittedly his hut was in a bit of a mess at the moment. A crate of empty beerbottles in the middle of the floor, with an empty flagon beside it and wet patches where beer had been spilt. Cigarette butts, matches and bottle tops that had missed the fireplace lay scattered around the hearth, and all that was left of the armfuls of firewood we'd brought in before dark was a heap of bark and some dead ashes in the grate. The lamp had gone out and a candle stuck in its own wax on the table was the only light.

There were three of us left, sitting round the table. Old Squinty, still wearing his too-big hat, with a nearly full bottle of whisky in front of him. Big Andy, who always wore a black bush-singlet. Dumb as hell and knew it. Always on the lookout for someone trying to put it across him because he was easy to put one across. Andy was okay as long as there was no funny business, and he never actually started any trouble. Just watched for it all the time and was far from slow over dealing with it when it came. And me, sitting there blankly watching him trying to roll a cigarette with one big end and tobacco hanging out of it everywhere.

It must have been about three in the morning and we'd been going well till the beer cut out and we started on the whisky. Now we were too bleary and tired to be bothered calling it a day.

The whisky bottle slid loudly across the table towards me. In the silence it sounded like a car crossing a loose cattle-stop.

"Have a beer," ordered Squinty, "and I won't hit you when you're drunk."

At the mention of hitting, Big Andy looked up interestedly, and as Squinty's meaning sank in he returned to his cigarette, which was in a worse mess than ever.

"It's not beer," I said. "It's bloody whisky." I raised the bottle and blew a few bubbles into it, letting a little of the stuff trickle into my mouth. Then I slid the bottle on round to Andy. The sliding of the bottle on the bare boards of the table had the nerve-grating effect of rusty tin on teeth, but it served to bring the next man's attention to the fact that it was his turn to force a drink down or admit he'd cut his load and couldn't take any more.

Andy raised the bottle in one huge paw, drank two noisy gulps, and banged it back on the table with a crack that interrupted me wondering whether old Squinty wore his big hat to bed or not.

"Bloody stuff," said Big Andy to nobody in particular. "Should have got another crate of beer."

"I know that," said Squinty. "Let's try a drop of me sister's honeymead. She sent me a bottle last Christmas and I've hardly touched it. It's real hot stuff."

Big Andy's interest revived at once at the mention of a new kind of drink, and mine at the idea of Squinty having a sister. He somehow didn't seem the kind of bloke who had relatives. A young Squinty was a hard thing to imagine, he'd been old for so long.

He rose stiffly to rummage in the dark corner cupboard and returned with a bottle three-quarters full of something that looked like thick sherry. He put it on the table and got an eight-ounce hotel glass from a shelf.

"Try some?" he asked, waving the glass in my direction.

"Not just now," I said quickly. "Think I'll stick to the whisky," I added, reaching for the bottle in front of Big Andy.

"I'll give it a go," said Andy superfluously.

Squinty uncorked the bottle with a loud *squick* and began to pour the honeymead into the glass.

"Say when," he said to Andy.

Andy still hadn't said anything when the glass was two-thirds full so Squinty stopped pouring.

"This'll do you for a start," he said, passing Andy the glass. "You've got to be careful how you handle this stuff. She'll burn holes in your singlet."

Andy raised the glass, looked at it for a moment, and then drained it in one smooth movement. Then he put the glass on the table and sat back to wait for the taste and results. Squinty and I watched for his reaction to this impressive performance. It wasn't long in coming.

His eyes screwed up, then opened wide and settled back to their normal bleariness. Without saying anything he looked back

153

and forth between me and Squinty as though he couldn't remember who we were. Then he reached a hairy arm past me and turned the label on the honeymead bottle towards the candle. It read:

Raw Linseed Oil
Leather Dressing
Not To Be Taken

Big Andy slowly put the bottle down and began to rise from his seat with a look on his face that left no doubt about what was going to happen to Squinty Bill — and me. Nothing was going to convince him that there hadn't been conspiracy between us to trick him into drinking linseed oil and he clearly intended "sewing us up", as he was in the habit of describing it, by way of preserving his pride. I sat helplessly watching, knowing that nothing I said was going to prevent a nasty beating up.

Then Squinty Bill, who'd been looking at the bottle with pursed lips, spoke.

"Wrong bottle, eh?" he said calmly. "Well, I don't give a guest in my camp anything to drink that I won't drink myself." And he grabbed the glass, poured himself a full eight ounces of Raw Linseed Oil and drank it in three gulps.

Big Andy stood half-crouched over his chair with a puzzled frown. Squinty took the whisky bottle, drank from it and passed it across to Andy.

"Better wash the taste out of your mouth," he said. "That oil's a hell of a brew."

Slowly Big Andy subsided back into his chair. Then, as though suddenly coming to a decision, he accepted the bottle

Squinty was holding out to him and drank a hefty slug.

"Sure is," he nodded.

The whole hut relaxed as Big Andy did. Even the candle seemed to perk up a little, but Squinty Bill gave no sign that he realised what had nearly happened. He got out the genuine bottle of honeymead — ghastly stuff it was — and we sat around the table drinking and waiting for the effects of the linseed oil to hit Squinty and Big Andy. But nothing happened, except that the more they drank the more sober they seemed to get.

We finished the bottle of whisky and by dawn I could scarcely keep my eyes open, while Andy and Squinty chatted over the last of the honeymead. The last thing I remember before going to sleep in my chair with my head on my arms was Squinty saying indignantly: "Y'know, Andy, that linseed oil hasn't got any kick in it. Doesn't make a bit of difference to a man."

And Big Andy replying sadly: "No. A man could drink it all night and not turn a hair."

"Shall we try a drop in the honeymead?" suggested Squinty.

"Yeah, good idea," said Andy brightly.

SEVENTEEN
That Way

Young Davey Hill was as keen on dogs as a starving tapeworm. He often had two or three hidden in the scrub along the big swamp and up the gully behind his father's homestead. Mongrels of all sizes and description that were surreptitiously fed from Davey's plate and late-night milkings of the house cow when he couldn't get scraps for them anywhere else. On an average of about once a month his father would hear Davey's dogs barking at night or catch him sneaking down to feed them, and another batch of stray mongrels would be released with a boot in the ribs and shouted and stoned off the place — on to somebody else's. Even Davey couldn't say where all these dogs came from. They just turned up and, in time, were turned out again.

Outbreaks of sheep-worrying were so prevalent that the farmers in the district took their rifles from porch corners almost as often as they put their old felt hats on. Old man Hill waited in apprehension for the phone to ring every time he heard a shot fired on a neighbouring property. Mr Hill was a very tolerant man, but when Davey turned fifteen and expressed a desire to leave school and home, he found it impossible to discourage the boy beyond pointing out the usual things about education and learning a trade. The Ringatu Rabbit Board won easily.

So two weeks and two phone calls after leaving high school Davey Hill left home with five dogs his father had never seen before and a shotgun that his father was never going to see again. He also had a lot of embarrassing last-minute advice and a bacon-and-egg pie from his wistful mother. His father drove him to the railway station in silence and there was more embarrassment while they waited for the train. Even the dogs were embarrassed.

The Ringatu Rabbit Board Inspector met Davey at the station and helped him load his dogs and gear into a Land Rover. He was a big easygoing bloke with a grin and a pipe. It was the first time Davey had ever been treated like a man; had someone bowl up to him, stick out his paw and say "Pleased to meet you, Dave, I'm Joe Scott. How did your dogs take the trip?"

As they drove madly along a road down the side of a gorge, talking about grown-up things like rainfall and erosion, Dave felt better about having left home.

"It's all dog and gun work out here," explained Joe. "We gave up the poison a couple of years ago. It's only a matter of keeping the old bunny down to where we've got him, now. We'll never get the last one or two, but we can't afford to let them breed up on us again. There'll be a Maori bloke in the hut up there with you. He's a bit rough on his dogs, old Kingi, but he's a bloody good rabbiter for all that. One of the best I've had yet. You'll find him okay to get along with."

The road left the bushed gorge and wound around into a valley that had been brought into pasture and divided into farms by the Government. You could still see patches of rank grass among the manuka and fern. The road from here on was strictly for Land Rovers.

"There's a couple of dairy farms at the head of the valley," said Joe. "They take all their stuff in and out the other way. This is only a short cut. All this country's going back. Bushsick as hell."

Dave didn't give a flax basket of kumaras whether the place was bushsick, lovesick, homesick or seasick. It looked pretty good to him.

Night and rain fell together as they arrived at the end of the clay track that led to Kingi Cooper's hut. He opened the door and stood like a lumpy statue against the light from a Tilley lamp on the ceiling behind him. Joe and Dave climbed out of the 'Rover, slammed the doors and went up onto the verandah of the hut.

"How's things, Kingi?" said Joe, following him inside.

"Been raining on and off all day. I worked some of the flats this morning and knocked off."

"That's the idea. There's no need to work in the rain — this is Dave Hill, he'll be giving you a hand up here for a while. Kingi — Dave."

Dave shook Kingi's big, engulfing hand and said hello.

Kingi was casually friendly. He was also the fairest-skinned Maori Dave had ever seen. In fact, he looked more like a slightly-curried European than a fair Maori. He gave Dave a hand to tie up his dogs while Joe unloaded the 'Rover.

"Where's your dogs, Kingi?" asked Dave as they walked back toward the hut in the rain.

"Got 'em tied up all over the place," replied Kingi. "You'll see enough of 'em in the morning."

Something about the place puzzled Dave. Something that wasn't quite right. It was only when he was lying in his bunk that night and Kingi and Joe were asleep that he realised what the something was. Dogs always kick up a hell of a racket when someone arrives, especially at night. There hadn't been a sound from Kingi's pack. And he was supposed to have fourteen of them.

Joe left them in the morning, which was fine, telling Kingi to ring him from a neighbouring farmer's place if they needed anything before he came again to pay them, in about two weeks' time.

Kingi and Dave set out to work a strip of country along a river beyond the hut. Dave's dogs were all over the place as soon as he let them off the chain, but not one of Kingi's left his heels before he told them to. He had everything from big scarred lurchers — all chest and legs — to pocket-sized burrow dogs. Terriers, spaniels and even a sheepdog. And not a pure-bred among them. Dave's dogs looked pretty much the same, but there the similarity ended. Kingi's pack was as highly trained as rabbit dogs can get. When he put them into a patch of cover the fast dogs spread out around it at places they instinctively knew were strategic, while the small hunting dogs dived into the fern or scrub and worked methodically through it. When a rabbit was driven out into the open it had little chance of getting far. The odd one or two that escaped into a burrow were guarded by the dogs until Kingi got there and threw a handful of granulated Cyanogas into the hole and dug in the entrance to seal the gas in. Dave shot a rabbit that doubled back past him and didn't let on how surprised he was to have hit it. He could see by this time why Kingi didn't bother carrying a shotgun. With his dogs he didn't need to.

Dave was a bit ashamed of his dogs, which were getting in the way all the time, but Kingi didn't say anything, so Dave decided he didn't mind.

Dave didn't want to knock off when it was time for them to work their way back towards the hut. They got eight rabbits for the day, which Kingi said was fairly average.

They fed the dogs from the carcase of a ram that was hanging in Kingi's dog-tucker tree with a piece of fencing-wire round its neck. That was how Kingi killed his dog-tucker rams.

The following afternoon when the dogs were chasing a rabbit round the side of a hill one of them started barking on the trail and Kingi seemed to be more interested in the dog than the rabbit.

"Poor old Wally. Never thought he'd go that way," he said, shaking his head sadly.

"Lots of dogs do that," said Dave.

"Not mine," said Kingi, and Dave remembered Joe's remark about Kingi being a bit rough on his dogs.

The dogs caught the rabbit and came struggling over to where the two men were leaning on a fence, one of them bringing the dead rabbit in its mouth. Kingi turned casually away from the fence and called Wally in.

"Here, Wally. Here, boy. There's a good dog now."

He began to pat the dog roughly on the ribs and then grabbed it by the muzzle with one hand and took out his sheath-knife with the other.

"Never thought you'd go that way," he said to the cringing dog as he doubled its head back, cut its throat and swung it into a clump of fern, almost in one movement. He wiped the knife on the thigh of his denims and stuck it back into its sheath.

Dave had turned away, his face as white as a cigarette paper and his ears roaring like surf. A silent circle of dogs stood twenty yards out from the fence. Dave led the way towards the next gully so Kingi wouldn't see his face. Kingi behaved as though nothing out of the ordinary had happened, which it hadn't; but Dave wasn't to know that. Kingi told a joke about a

160

bullock-driver, but he had to do all the laughing himself. Dave had just noticed that the band of blood on Kingi's trousers where he'd wiped the knife wasn't the only one.

A few days later they drove to a farm in Kingi's old truck to get a dog-tucker cow the farmer had left a note in their hut about. The cocky was in the middle of his milking when they arrived at the cowshed.

"I've got the old girl in the yard here," he said, leading the way past cud-chewing, muddy-legged cows to the back of the yard, where the sick cow drooped near the rails.

"The vet says she's a gonner. Been going down in condition for a couple of weeks. Not much left on her, but she might be worth a feed or two for your dogs. We'll put her out into the paddock so you can shoot her and. . ."

"This'll do," interrupted Kingi, running one hand along the cow's bony spine. Then he had his knife out and her throat cut before the farmer or Dave realised what he was doing. While they watched in silence Kingi held the cow against the rail until she sank to her knees and rolled over, kicking feebly. Then he stooped to wipe his knife on the quivering rump.

The other cows began to stir around the yard, bellowing and snorting at the scent of blood. Cows stirred and stamped in the bails. A set of cups fell off and lay sucking noisily on the wet concrete. One by one the other three sets of cups fell and were trampled by restless feet. Dave and the farmer looked a little wild-eyed at each other and then at Kingi, who was steeling his knife to begin skinning.

"I think you've lost a lot of cups mate," he said, glancing at the cocky. "Give us a hand to roll her over, Dave."

Dave went over and pulled weakly at a hind leg. The cocky shut off the vacuum in the pipes and began to let the rest of his cows out through the shed. He had as much show of getting milk from bulls, the state his cows were in. He went up to the house without another word to the two rabbiters.

As they drove away with the quarters of meat glowing on the back of the truck, Kingi said: "I think he's a bit annoyed with us for upsetting his cows. How the hell were we to know they'd go that way?"

In the two weeks that followed, Dave managed to get away on his own most of the time and work blocks of country that were too small and patchy for it to be worth two men doing. His dogs were getting good at the work and he didn't miss many rabbits. Through not having any fast dogs, he had to rely on his shotgun a fair bit. Occasionally Kingi would come back to camp with one less dog than he left with and sadly explain that Biddy or Whisky or Nigger had "gone that way". Dave was so uncomfortable in his presence that it was a relief to get out on the job in the mornings, where he could forget about Kingi in the enjoyment of the work and watching his dogs improving.

Joe came, paid them and went.

Then there was the horse. An old station packhorse that they were to shoot for the dogs with a .303 rifle Joe had left with them for the job. They pulled up at the gate of the paddock with all the dog-tucker gear on the back of Kingi's truck. Sacks, rope, shovel, steel hooks, gambels and axes. The horse had seen them coming and came and hung its tired old head over the fence to see if there was anything to do or to eat or only to watch. Dave sat in the truck and said to Kingi: "You can shoot him. I'm not much good with a three-O."

"She's right," said Kingi. "I think I'll be able to catch him."

"No," said Dave, getting quickly out and grabbing for the rifle. "I'll shoot it."

But Kingi was already walking towards the horse. Dave watched as he stroked the nuzzling head and ran a hand down the horse's neck. Then he climbed up the fence and over onto its back, speaking quietly to it. The horse turned and began to walk along the fence to the gate, with Kingi sitting on its back steeling his knife. From where he was sitting, it took him four slashes to get its throat properly cut. Dave could hear the blood pouring into the ground as the horse wandered in an aimless little circle. When it went down, Kingi stepped off and deftly wiped his knife on the hide as the horse rolled over to kick out the last of its life in the mud it had made walking up and down the fence, waiting in case it was needed.

It was then that Dave began to really hate Kingi.

The next day one of Dave's dogs barked on the trail when Kingi was there.

"That Ruff of yours barking on the trail, eh?"

"Yeah."

"Never thought he'd go that way."

"No."

"Got your knife on you?"

"No, I haven't."

"I'll fix him for you. Here, Ruff. Here boy. There's a good dog . . ."

Dave just watched.

Joe came, paid them and left.

Three more dogs, a horse, two rams and a cow.

Joe came, paid them and left. They caught the Rabbit Board's old packhorse that had been turned out for the winter in a cocky's back paddock and loaded him up for a trip to a hut in the hills beyond the river. It was an area that had to be given a rake-over every three months or so. They crossed the river and let the creaking horse lead the way up a side valley to a slab hut in the tussock, four hours from the base hut.

They worked all their country in eight days. Every morning Dave shifted the packhorse to a new stake-out and occasionally cut a bit of extra grass for him. Kingi cut another dog's throat for coming into the hut after it had been chased out. Dave was getting so good with his shotgun that Kingi, who was against their use, admitted that it was handy to have sometimes. He had only seven dogs left and Dave had four.

They were loading their stuff into pack-boxes for the trip back to the base hut when two of the dogs started fighting outside. One of Dave's and one of Kingi's. Dave ran out and grabbed a hind leg but Kingi didn't need his help. He stuck his boot on one dog's neck and grabbed the other by the muzzle. While the two dogs struggled and squirmed he took out his knife with his free hand and tested the edge with his thumb. Then he doubled back the head of the dog in his hand . . .

Blood sprayed up his sleeve and across the back of his coat. Then he bent to wipe his knife, on the ribs of Dave's dog under his foot, before giving it a few casual rubs on the steel. Then he took the dog by the muzzle. Dave turned away.

They headed for the base and it was getting late by the time they reached the river. Kingi caught up the packhorse and climbed on top of the load to save getting his feet wet on the river crossing. Dave stood on the bank and watched the horse stagger to its overloaded knees among the boulders in the river. One of Kingi's feet, which he'd tucked into the pack-straps, went right through as he came off. The horse plunged through the water and on to the rocks across the river and stood snorting at the scent of blood on Kingi's coat. His foot was still wedged between the pack-strap and the load. He reached up to free himself, talking quietly to the horse. Dave couldn't hear what he was saying, but he knew well enough. Never thought you'd go that way . . .

Dave raised his shotgun and quietly cocked the hammer behind the choke barrel. He knew exactly where to aim. At that range it was easy. The number four shot pattern burnt the horse neatly across the rump. It only took the terrified animal a few seconds to reach a bend in the river and stumble and plunge around the corner out of sight. Kingi looked like a rag man, bouncing along among the boulders and hooves.

It was too late to go for help that night. First thing in the morning he'd do all the things you're supposed to do when there's an accident in the back country.

At ten o'clock that night Dave threw the dregs of his tea into the sizzling fireplace and went out to have a yarn with the dogs; to tell them everything was okay now. When the cold had drawn all the heat from the fire out of his clothes he gave the dogs a last pat each and went inside for another mug of tea.

Kingi was standing there. With all his weight on one leg and his back to the fire. He seemed somehow to be all out of shape. Something had happened to his nose and forehead. He opened his mouth to grin but it didn't look very funny.

"Didn't think you'd go that way, boy."

166

EIGHTEEN

HORSEPLAY

My first impression of Laura Trumble was that she would have liked to be able to crawl away somewhere and hide till the rest of her life blew over. She would stand with her hands clutched apprehensively in front of her as though she'd just come from the scene of an accident that she wasn't quite sure whether or not she was responsible for. Interviews with her were like dreams, it was hard to be sure whether they'd actually taken place. Whenever you spoke to her she'd nod her head up and down, depending on how quickly you spoke, as though your words were bouncing from floor to ceiling. And when she spoke to you it was as though she was in a library; as though she was afraid of frightening you away, so you had to lean and listen to catch what she was saying. And her eyes opened and closed in time with her mouth, and you were so fascinated by this that you forgot to listen to what she was saying anyway.

The only time anybody seemed to really notice what Laura said was when she came out with something outrageous that threw everyone out of gear. It wouldn't have been so if she could have covered up, but she'd lost faith in lies years before and never trusted them. There was something precarious about her, a kind of anxiety, as though she'd just passed you a poem she wrote to her first boyfriend when she was thirteen. Or as though she'd just felt some elastic give way on her.

Another thing about Laura Trumble was that she seemed to me to be always trying not to look like an emu. But it never worked. In her best clothes she looked like a dressed-up emu. In her working clothes she looked like a working emu. If she grew her hair long she looked like an emu with long hair, and if she cut it short she looked like an emu with a haircut. Sometimes she even experimented with a home perm, but it only made her look like a moulting emu. For months I had the absurd conviction that if she was to get angry with me she'd reach out her long neck and peck me in the face, so that my left eye would twitch embarrassingly whenever I was talking or listening to her.

I understood that she'd been married until six or seven years before. It seemed that her husband left his car at a garage one day and asked them to check his brakes. The man from the garage ran over him in his own car when he was crossing the street half an hour later and he died of his injuries. Laura moved to Talltree Point and had lived ever since on her thirty-five acres in an old brown house that looked as though it had actually grown up through the fern and long grass that clung thickly around its walls and windows. She usually wore long trousers, gumboots, and a big straw hat, and although she spent most of her time outdoors, she was the only one in Talltree Point who never got sunburnt, even in the summer. It was as though the sun had been ordered to leave her alone.

This, then, was Laura Trumble, the best man with animals that anyone who had ever met her had ever met.

She could take careless cats and have them thoroughly house-trained in two days. In one visit to the cowshed she could stop a new-calved heifer holding its milk. In two days she could teach a dog to sit, come here and fetch. She could have a magpie saying "Hello" and "Aakawarrk" in less than a week. Even the trout in the little creek that ran through her place would come to

168

be fed scraps when she swished her hand in the water and called them. She was the only one who could get Wally Catch's big bull into the crush when they had to put a ring in its nose to stop it smashing fences. When everyone else had given up trying, she could stop horses from bucking, biting, kicking and bolting. She was the only one who could catch Sam Steven's racehorse the time it ate tutu along the creek and got poisoned and went mad. She was the only one who could do anything with Bill Sutton's Jersey bull the time it went mad from fighting Rod Norton's Shorthorn through the fence and all the fat in its head melted. She spoke to animals in hypnotic whispers, soothed and smoothed and sorted out whatever was troubling them. Ripped pig-dogs that couldn't be stitched up; half-wild bullocks, bloated from breaking into clovery paddocks; sheep-worried dogs and dog-worried sheep; cows in bogs and pigs in trouble. Laura Trumble fixed them all. She had needles and bandages and plaster and splints, knives and liniment, warm sheds, soft hay, advice and comfort. Anything that had to do with animals she could do better than anyone else. Even the veterinary man from over at Swinton used to come and collect Laura when he had a tricky job on. It was often said that if Laura Trumble was anybody but Laura Trumble she'd be a famous animal handler for a big circus, or a zoo or something. As it was she was just Laura Trumble.

It was a hot afternoon the July before last and a few of us were yarning around in the shade of Bruce Walter's garage when a bloke in a big flash Chrysler pulled up beside the petrol-pump and told Bruce to fill 'er up. It took not quite thirteen gallons and we all had to take it in turns to work the pump handle. Then the bloke asked where he could find Mrs Laura Trumble. We pointed out Laura's place and he drove off down there. A couple of hours later he whirled back past the garage without stopping and it was over a week before we found out what he'd come for, Laura not being much of a one to pass on information.

It turned out that the stranger was Carl Middleton, the big racehorse owner. It seems he'd spent thousands of dollars importing a thoroughbred brood mare from England, and more thousands breeding a foal from her. The foal was now a rising four-year-old stallion and nobody could get near it, let alone do anything with it. The experts had finally pronounced that the horse was mad. It wasn't even safe to put it in with valuable brood mares. It was going to have to be destroyed. Then Carl Middleton had heard about our Laura Trumble from the veterinary man at Swinton's brother-in-law, and he'd come to see her as a last resort.

The horse arrived in a big horsebox on the back of a truck. You could hear it kicking at the sides of the box as they went past the garage. Carl Middleton drove along in front in his flash car. They pulled up at Laura's place and she and two men walked around her house paddock inspecting the fences. Then they backed the truck into the paddock and one of the men climbed up to open the door of the swaying horsebox. Everyone else got back through the gate out of the way. The door fell open, making a ramp from the truck down to the ground. And the stallion, a beautiful big bay, about sixteen hands, backed kicking out of the horsebox and half fell off the side of the ramp. Then it leapt, plunged and galloped out into the paddock. It was amazing that he hadn't broken a leg or something.

The stallion was mad all right. He stood there, quivering and

snorting, for a few moments and then whirled and galloped, bucking and flinging himself in all directions at once, the full length of the paddock. Just when it looked as though he was going to tear right through the macrocarpa hedge behind the fence at the bottom of the paddock, he propped, skidded a good fifteen yards and wheeled along the fence, bucking and rearing and snorting as though the Devil himself was on his back. At the far corner he stopped and stood with his head drooping and the wind whistling in his nostrils. Then suddenly he squealed and reared and galloped again along the bottom fence to the corner, where he turned to gallop back again, all the time keeping up his crazy bucking and lashing-out.

Laura took Carl Middleton and his men into the house and a couple of hours later they came out and drove away. The stallion was resting a little between his mad fits of running and jumping around, but any activity around the place was enough to set him up in business again.

All that night the mad stallion galloped up and down the fence at the bottom of Laura Trumble's house-paddock. By morning he'd churned a great muddy track along the fence that we could easily see from the garage. We began to wonder when he was going to collapse from sheer exhaustion. He was settling down for longer periods now, and even cropping a few crops of grass now and then, but whenever anyone came within sight of him he'd set up his running-plunging act again and keep it up for long after they were gone.

Now all of us around Talltree Point began to notice how proud of Laura Trumble we were. I suppose we'd been taking her a fair bit for granted. Anyway there was a lot of indignation about this bloke Middleton landing her with this impossible animal. There

172

was some talk of asking the police over at Swinton to order the horse taken away again for Laura's safety. The outcome of it was that we all sat back and waited to see what Laura was going to do with the mad stallion.

And she did nothing. Absolutely nothing. She didn't even keep out of his way, but strutted like a busy emu through and around the paddock whenever she felt like it, completely ignoring the frantic contortions the stallion flew into whenever she appeared. She didn't even look at him, even when he came plunging and snorting along the fence towards her. She just strolled along towards the gate with her bucket of milk, and when the stallion got to within a few yards of her he stopped, snorted and wheeled back along the fence. Not only did Laura do nothing about the mad horse, but she went on doing nothing. For week after week.

And the horse couldn't take it. He got to going through his act right in front of her as she passed through the paddock, but she refused to even look. He ran after her but she ignored his presence as though he didn't exist. He took to coming closer to the house and eventually stood for hours with his head over the yard gate, waiting for her to come out so he could try and impress her. But she went on doing nothing about it. He started running ahead of her across the paddock and then even following her, getting closer and closer to her, but he was wasting his time.

Just as the mad horse got to getting closer to Laura, some of us got to getting closer to the horse. Just about every day one or two of us'd go down to Laura's gate and lean there, looking and saying what we thought might be done with it. The horse ignored us altogether after a while, and Laura went on ignoring the horse.

Carl Middleton and one of his men came to see how Laura was getting on with their stallion, and he turned on one of his best performances for them. They talked to Laura at the gate for a while and then drove back past the garage, looking grim.

And with Laura going on ignoring the horse he actually started to fret and look pathetic over the fence while she fed all her other animals in the next paddock and patted them and talked to them. He gave himself the job of escorting Laura safely across his paddock, walking along beside her, bursting for attention — and not getting it. He pretended to get a fright sometimes and bolt down the paddock, but it wasn't very convincing. Nobody ever actually mentioned the horse to Laura and she never talked about him, so we were pretty hard pushed for conversation sometimes.

Six weeks after his last visit, Carl Middleton, with three other men this time, arrived at Laura's place. The mad horse went mad and they went inside and stayed there for about an hour and a half. Then they left.

Then one day Laura left the gate open and the horse followed her across to the hay-barn and over to where the cows were being fed. He ate a bit of hay and followed her back into his own paddock. The day after that I called in to ask Laura to marry me, and there was the stallion, in the yard of the house, eating the long grass. I froze in my tracks and then he saw me. He raised his head, looked at me for a moment, and then went on eating, swishing his tail at the flies.

That day I came straight out and asked Laura when she was going to start breaking in the horse and would she like me to help. But she just said that he was coming along nicely. It was over a month before I found out that Carl Middleton had given

Laura the horse for what he owed her for grazing and time she'd wasted. He'd given up any hope of ever getting the thing quietened down. He'd even made it legal so that he wouldn't be responsible for any damage the horse did.

And that's how Laura came to be the owner of one of the best-bred horses in the country, although you wouldn't think so to look at him. He's covered with mud and his mane's all tangled and full of burrs. And the calves have chewed his tail all to wisps. As a matter of fact he's a bit of a nuisance these days. Keeps getting in the way all the time.

We've got Joe Dobbie's draught mare in foal to him, and Wally Catch's grey hack (but we're not absolutely certain yet). We would actually make a fair bit of money with him serving brood-mares, but the wife wouldn't hear of it.

I haven't much say in the matter really. After all it was her who went to all the trouble of getting him.

NINETEEN
WARM BEER

The short cut across the hills turned out to be a lousy idea. Old Sniffer climbed across the third gully and up to the crest of the fourth ridge. The road he was looking for wasn't in that gully either. Only a straggly sheeptrack wound its way aimlessly across the opposite hillside as though it had been drawn there by a child with a pencil.

He stood looking around the overgrown countryside, sweating beerily in the last of the still sunshine. A sheep bleated somewhere but he couldn't see any sheep, or anything at all except the desertedness of everything.

Already he was beginning to recognise the symptoms of an unfairly premature hangover. It was less than an hour since he'd left the pub. He wiped his face on the sleeve of his shirt and started down the hillside towards the bottom of the gully, where shadows were beginning to lie around, like something spilt and spreading.

It was almost gloomy down in the gully and he was feeling the faint remainder of his old knee. He looked up the slope he had to climb and then at the old road that lay half-submerged in the ferns along the floor of the dry gully. It wasn't the road he was looking for, but maybe it joined it farther down. He began to push his way, limping a little now because of his knee, along the muddy, patchy, overgrown road.

Soon he could hear water trickling in the tiny stream under the fern and scrub just below the road. He began to look for a way down to it, rolling a dried-up gob of saliva uselessly around in his parched mouth. Then the road, if it could be called that, opened out into what had once been a sizeable clearing. He saw the burnt-out remains of what had been a fairly big house, and a few posts and rails rotting in a scattered heap. Stockyards of some kind. Another old house, more like a shack, this one, only a dried skeleton of warped boards and framework. It must have been years since anyone was here.

Old Sniffer looked around, a little bewildered at finding this remote place within such a short time of leaving a pub full of people. He sat on a lump of turf, which turned out to be an old anvil overgrown with weeds and grass, and wondered what the hell to do. It was getting really dark now, and he was obviously miles from anywhere. He was going to have to spend the night in this godforsaken place and probably be crippled up with another dose of rheumatism for a couple of weeks until he drank it out of his bones again. It was then, in the shadowy, creeping dark of the tumbling hidden valley, that he saw, flung carelessly out on a little rise at the foot of a descending ridge, the scattered broken headstones of a long-ago graveyard.

A dirty angel with spread wings swooped eternally into a great clump of fern, and stumpy streaky head stones of all shapes and sizes reared, reached, peered, leaned and lumbered around among the falling fences of the half-acre or so of this astonishing place.

Sniffer pushed his way curiously in the gloom through the undergrowth up the rise, till he stood at the edge of the graveyard. His eyes had grown slightly accustomed to the dark and he pushed his way towards a falling headstone and was bending down to peer at the inscription on it when a voice beside him said helpfully:

"Wattie Beamish. Died eighteen eighty-four from an overdose of nagging. Not a bad bloke when you got to know him. He's on afternoon-shift heart-attacks this week."

Sniffer turned to gaze in astonishment at his informer. A fair-dinkum ghost. Absolutely normal-looking in every respect, except that he was slouching with all his weight leaning against a shimmery frond of fern. He looked as though he'd just stepped off a bus on his way home from work, or something. Sniffer was a bit knocked back by all this, and, perhaps excusably, just stood there gaping. The ghost went on:

"It's not often we get visitors here these days. Forty years ago we almost had to give this place up altogether, there were so many people about. — Sit down." And he set an example by drifting over and perching lightly on the raised edge of Wattie Beamish's grave. Sniffer obediently sat beside him, as far away as he could politely get.

"Er, what are you doing here?" asked Sniffer, for the sake of something to say.

"I'm on guide duty," said the ghost. "Most of us have to put in a few years guiding at first."

"What about the women?" asked Sniffer. He was trying, for some reason, to keep the conversation on this harmless level.

"Oh we don't have much to do with them," explained the ghost. "We ghosts aren't interested in sex, and without it women aren't much use to us. They're kept in a different place altogether. I believe some of 'em are quite useful in some ways. They've got some kind of training scheme going now, you know. — Would you care for a beer?"

"Well, yes. I wouldn't mind one," said Sniffer thirstily. "Have you got any?" he added suspiciously.

"Sure," said the ghost, producing a bottle of beer from some invisible where. "Not a bad drop the Northern Brewery turns out these days." He flipped the top off the bottle with an enormous opener and passed it to Sniffer. "Got this from a car accident a few minutes ago. Bloke won't be needing it where he's going. Nothing'll make a man crook quicker than warm beer."

"Thanks," said Sniffer. And he carefully took the bottle and drank several hefty gulps of genuine Northern Bitter.

"A bit frothy," observed the ghost, taking the bottle from Sniffer. "It's been shaken up a bit."

"Perhaps you could tell me where the main road is from here," said Sniffer. "I've lost my direction coming over those hills there."

"Roads?" said the ghost as though he wasn't quite sure what they were. "Oh yes. Never use 'em myself. They always seem to go the long way round. I have seen one or two somewhere round here, but I couldn't tell you where one is off-hand, though."

"Doesn't really matter," said Sniffer, taking the bottle again, which he noticed was still nearly full. "I just wanted to get to my hut over on the main road. Tried to take a short cut but I got a bit lost."

"If you want to borrow Wattie's grave here for a snore-off till he gets off work, I'm sure he won't mind," said the ghost helpfully.

"No, thanks all the same," said Sniffer quickly. "I'm not at all tired. It's just that I wanted to get home sometime tonight. Thanks for the offer, though."

"Don't mention it," said the ghost pleasantly. "We can always dig you up a bunk here if you're stuck. — What have they got

you doing for a crust these days?"

"Roadman," said Sniffer, passing back the bottle. "Due to retire next year. What about you?"

"Just guide duty. I'm on road accidents at the moment. Hardly enough business to keep us going lately. We get most of our business in the holiday season, you know. Thanks — good luck. So you're due to retire, eh?"

"Yep, I'll be sixty-five next October."

"Well, I don't suppose it'll be long before we'll be seeing you down at headquarters."

"What do you mean by that?" demanded Sniffer.

"Oh, it's always the same," said the ghost with a wave of his hand. "Once they retire they don't last long. Of course we've got one or two little lurks to help things along. Nothing drastic, you understand; a bit of rheumatism during the winter; shut down on the eyesight here and there — increases the possibility of falling down stairs and things like that, y'know — and then, of course, there's always the old booze. That helps a lot, especially in cases like yours. It's really quite surprising how you can boost your tally if you put your mind to it."

Sniffer put the bottle down on the edge of the grave. "You can cut that out, mate," he said belligerently. "I didn't come here to be knocked off by rheumatism and booze. I'm as fit as any bloke half my age. I've got years left in me yet."

"No need to get shirty," said the ghost. "You've all got to go sometime."

"Well I'm not going till I'm good and ready," said Sniffer hotly. "And that's that."

"We've got pretty good conditions here now, you know. Not like the old days."

"I don't give a damn what you've got," insisted Sniffer. "I'm hanging on here as long as I can, and I've got years to go yet."

"Good prospects for promotion, according to ability and length of service," quoted the ghost. "That means that if you join us now, by nineteen ninety-six . . ."

"I'm not joining you now or any other time."

"Come now. Let's be realistic about this. You've got to come sometime — why not make it now? It's all shift work these days, you know. Time and a half for Saturday mornings and double time Sundays and public holidays. Interesting variety. Only one day a month on hospital duty. Superannuation. — Think what you'll be passing up. The longer you stay here. . ."

"No," said Sniffer definitely, drinking again from the bottle and passing it back to the ghost.

"But think of three weeks' annual leave on full pay," said the ghost eagerly.

"Not impressed," said Sniffer.

"The union intends going to a forty-hour-week at the next annual general meeting of the Federation of . . ."

"You're wasting your time," interrupted Sniffer. "I'm not going, and that's final."

"That's too bad," said the ghost, drinking resignedly from the bottle and tossing it empty into the fern, "because I've come to take you in. I always try to make it as easy as possible, but you'd be surprised how stubborn people can be about a simple little thing like that."

"Well, you're not taking me anywhere," said Sniffer. "It might be simple to you, but I've got used to it here. I'm not ready to retire yet, anyway. I'd get the sack if I just walked out on the job like that without telling them. Why, I'd probably lose my old age pension over it. I'd never get another job with the county, that's for sure. Besides, it'd be hard on an old man to change his habits after a lifetime. He gets set in his ways, you know. It could affect his health. And what about my back pay? They wouldn't know where to send it. And what about my working gear? They dock your pay if you just leave without handing it in. And there's a lot of things I haven't finished. And . . ."

But the ghost insisted.